Tales of Scotland Yard:

Ratcliffe Highway

by Bianca Jenkins

Paperback ISBN 978-1-80424-530-9
ePub ISBN 978-1-80424-531-6
PDF ISBN 978-1-80424-532-3

Published by MX Publishing - Orange Pip Books
335 Princess Park Manor, Royal Drive, London, N11 3G
www.orangepipbooks.com

Cover design by Awan

One

Superintendent Hilton Beals sat at his desk, working his way through what felt like a never-ending mountain of paperwork. He did not look up as a knock sounded at his office door, neither did he pause in his writing.

"Come." The door opened to admit a younger man dressed in a dark suit. "Leave it open," Beals added, when the recent arrival made as if to close the door behind him.

"Yes, sir." The prompt reply went unacknowledged as the man crossed the room, coming to stand in front of his superior's desk.

Beals let him stand there.

Beals had found, over the years, the tactic was an excellent way to get a man's measure. Time and time again the superintendent had learned nearly everything he needed to know about his men simply by making them wait after he called them to his office. Some men grew impatient and fidgeted, some grew angry, some grew anxious. The longer he made them wait the more a man's personality, failures and flaws included, made their way to the surface.

The man currently standing in front of his desk stood carefully at attention, as was appropriate for his lesser rank. He also remained silent, seemingly willing to accept that his superintendent knew he was there, and was clearly not yet ready to speak to him. This one, at least, seemed to understand how to act around his superiors.

Now Beals stopped writing. Carefully he set aside his pen, as well as the completed form. After a moment's consideration, he picked up a new sheet of paper and began reading. Through all this the man standing before him remained in place, never so much as shifting his balance as he waited to be acknowledged.

Beals let this go on for several more minutes, but the man standing before him did not seem inclined to fidget, or sigh, or even so much as look around the room while his superior ignored him. Finally, Beals set aside his paper.

"Lestrade, was it?" he asked, looking over his newest inspector.

They had not officially met. Not yet. Beals rarely bothered with the rookies, not until they proved they could make it through their first few months without getting themselves killed out of sheer stupidity. This one, if the reports were accurate, may have suffered more than his fair share of stupidity, but had at least demonstrated an ability not to get himself killed too quickly.

"Yes, sir." The man was respectful, at least.

Lestrade wore a dark, three piece suit that was, even to Beals' inexperienced eye, both high quality and made to last. His shoes were equally well made. He was better dressed than any of the other inspectors at Scotland Yard-better dressed than even Beals himself currently was. More impressive, he was also far cleaner than any man who had been out and about in the city that day had any right to be.

The inspector was *short,* the superintendent realized, and spent a moment eyeballing the man, not entirely convinced he was actually tall enough to meet the height requirement for the London police, before continuing his inspection.

Lestrade's height, when coupled with his slight build, should have made him look like an easy target, a dangerous thing for a policeman, but something about the way he carried himself even now, while standing at attention in his pretty little suit, said otherwise. It was subtle, and at a first glance might have been easily missed, but there nonetheless. This dapper little man knew how to handle himself.

Lestrade still did not move-or speak-as the superintendent continued to look him over, and Beals found himself wondering almost absently if the man would utter so much as a word without prompting. He took in the inspector's sallow and pinched complexion and also wondered if he had been ill lately, or if the young inspector always looked like that.

Their eyes met; Lestrade did not look away. His dark, nearly black eyes seemed to take in everything about the man standing before him, and for a moment, Superintendent Beals felt as if *he* were the one being evaluated.

Whatever those eyes saw, the inspector's expression gave away none of it. Polite, bland-but not quite bored-Lestrade could have rivaled any servant or shop-keeper's professional demeanor. It had the potential to serve him well in dealing with his betters-both inside the Yard and out, except for one thing: when combined with eyes that seemed to see too much, he looked more secretive than trustworthy.

"You've been an inspector how long?" Beals broke the silence abruptly, but did not catch Lestrade off guard.

"Four months, sir."

"And how long have you been with the police in general?" he pressed.

"Six years, Superintendent."

4

"You were assigned to Inspector Johnson after your promotion?"

"Yes, sir."

"And you encouraged him to investigate the disappearances of six children, leading to the arrest of a gang of slave-traders and the loss of one of our own men, correct?"

Lestrade blinked. "Sir?"

Beals raised his eyebrows. "Inspector Matthew Flint was among the men arrested. Were you aware that one of the men you helped capture was a member of Scotland Yard and an *inspector,* no less*?"*

"Yes, sir." Lestrade's face remained carefully blank, but he shifted his weight ever so slightly as he answered.

"Explain yourself."

This time Lestrade's brows furrowed in confusion. "Sir?"

Beals leaned back in his chair, steepling his fingers together as he watched the younger man. "I'd like an explanation for your involvement in the case. Why you thought it was a good idea to take on a case without your senior officer's knowledge, or his permission. Why you pursued the matter, in spite of Inspector Johnson warning against it. Why you continued even when it appeared that one of your fellow inspectors might be involved."

Lestrade stared at the man for a moment, then gathered himself.

"Nobody else was willing to listen to the mother of the most recent victim," he offered, his voice low but steady. "Her son was missing, and it's our job to help people-"

Beals raised an eyebrow. "Are you trying to tell me my job?" he asked, mainly to see what the younger man would do.

Lestrade shook his head. "No, sir. But you asked what I was thinking. I couldn't turn her away, not when we're supposed to help. I didn't intend to get caught up in a kidnapping ring, Superintendent, but when we found the missing child at the morgue, the doctor there mentioned that there had been other children found, matching the same description. Inspector Johnson realized it had to be slave-traders."

"And he wanted to hunt them down, naturally." Beals suggested, the words fairly dripping with sarcasm.

"No, sir," Lestrade looked surprised. "He warned against it, but-" here Lestrade hesitated. "Even if it were dangerous, Superintendent, it was still our responsibility to try to find the people responsible – wasn't it? Isn't it?"

For the first time, a hint of emotion leaked through Lestrade's carefully constructed mask, though only his eyes gave him away. Fear shone in those dark eyes. Fear and just a hint of desperation, as if Lestrade had suddenly realized that Flint might not have been the only corrupt policeman in the world, and that his superior might not agree with his assessment of the situation.

Beals was a practical man. He was not particularly dishonest himself, or so he believed, but he was well aware of the rampant corruption that had taken root in Scotland Yard since even before his time, and he knew that fighting that corruption could get a man killed.

So he had kept his head down and minded his own business. When it became necessary, he acted. After years of walking a very fine line, he had somehow managed to stay clean enough (without causing trouble for the other, somewhat less morally upstanding inspectors he worked with) to be considered for promotion. He had taken it, telling himself that he could at least do damage control even if he couldn't really fix anything, and in the past ten years had done little more than sit in his office and pretend to turn a blind eye to the doings of his fellow policemen.

Beals considered the man standing before him for a long moment. "Your desire to do what's right is admirable, Lestrade," he said, not unkindly. "But you need to understand that what is right and what is reality are not always the same thing. Just because something *should* be a certain way, doesn't mean it will be. The real world doesn't often work like that, unfortunately."

Lestrade did not look away, and because he did not the other man saw quite clearly the betrayal that flashed in his eyes for an instant before they, like the rest of his expression, blanked.

"Yes, sir," Lestrade said, but he did not sound as if he meant it.

Beals let the matter rest. Sometimes a man needed time to digest the advice of older, more experienced men, especially when he did not like it. "Your first solo case was a murder?"

"Yes, sir." Lestrade could not quite banish the resentment from his voice. "The woman was murdered by her husband in front of several witnesses. He confessed when we questioned him."

"Good work," Beals told him. "*That* is the kind of police work we like to see. Straightforward. Clear. No muddling about with conspiracies, no shadows cast on the reputations of any of our own people. "These are the kind of cases that will prove your worth as an inspector and help you go far in your chosen profession."

"Yes, sir." A beat. "Thank you, sir."

Beals smiled at the man. "Keep up the good work, Lestrade." It was meant more as a warning than as encouragement. He picked up his pen to see if Lestrade would take the gesture as a dismissal, but the inspector never moved.

"Dismissed, Lestrade," he said, thinking to himself. *He's obedient in all the wrong ways, and willful in all the worst.*

"Yes, sir." Lestrade left, closing the door carefully behind him.

Beals stared absently at the empty space in which the man had recently stood, the pen forgotten in his hand, his paperwork all but abandoned, his mind going over what he had just learned about Scotland Yard's newest inspector.

Lestrade worried him.

"Still alive, I see." Inspector Smith joked as Lestrade reached the hall where his office was located. The man was of average height and build, which meant Lestrade had to look up to meet his eyes even as the other inspector leaned on the wall next to an open office door, waiting for the younger man to return. Light eyes met dark good-naturedly; Smith genuinely liked the strange little inspector standing before him, even if he did not always understand him.

"Sir?" Smith was, by now, almost completely certain that in spite of the question Lestrade did, in fact, get the joke. Whether or not the feigned ignorance was simply a matter of reflex he was less certain. It was possible the younger inspector still felt wary of his colleagues, but Smith would have hoped that by this point the man would have loosened up just a little.

Smith shrugged. Rather than explain, he asked, "So how did it go? Superintendent chew you to bits?"

There was a split second of delay while Lestrade debated how to answer, and his fellow inspector felt vindicated when the man offered an actual reply instead of further prevarication.

"He asked about the case with Flint," Lestrade said. "He wanted an explanation for my actions," he did not offer details. "He also explained what kind of cases he expects me to work in the future, if I want to do well here." Lestrade's voice was carefully neutral, but Smith knew better by now than to think the other inspector was unbothered by the conversation.

"I remember being told what kind of work the superintendent expects of me," Smith said comfortably from his place against the wall. "I wouldn't worry too much about it."

A snort from inside the open door to Smith's right revealed that the two were not alone. Lestrade turned to find Inspector Adams seated at his desk, shaking his head at his fellow policeman's assertion.

"I would hope you remember. That conversation happened *yesterday* when he called you into his office over that mugging you stumbled across." To Lestrade he said, "Beals is a lot of talk and very little action. He's not crooked himself, exactly, but he's not going to risk his position or his life to try to clean house. It's just not worth it."

Though thinner than Smith, Adams too was of average height, with brown eyes and a far more serious outlook on life. He wasn't sure he liked Lestrade, but he did at least know he could trust the man. Lestrade had proved that much within the first month of his arrival at Scotland Yard.

Inspector Johnson, sitting across the desk from Adams, shook his head. Tall and lean with dark hair and gray eyes, Johnson was the oldest of the bunch, and the man Lestrade had been partnered with after his promotion to Inspector. Even now, four months later, Johnson tended to keep an eye out for the younger man, offering advice when he felt it was needed and worrying every time Lestrade looked like he might clash with one of the inspectors outside of their small group.

Johnson, Smith, and Adams had all been heavily involved in the slave-trading case the superintendent had asked Lestrade about. Out of all the policemen at Scotland Yard, they had been the only ones willing to get involved, and the only ones Lestrade had been able to trust.

They were still the only men he willingly talked to, though that was admittedly only when one of them initiated a conversation; Lestrade himself had never been much of a talker. He had by now met most of the other inspectors at Scotland Yard; they had introduced themselves one by one as they decided he had been around long enough to take notice of, but beyond that they had taken little interest in him, and Lestrade preferred to keep it that way.

He could have made enemies after the slave-trading case; Matthew Flint had been well liked by most of his colleagues. Lestrade had been fortunate that even the more questionable of the policemen at the Yard seemed to take issue with kidnapping and child-murder.

"Just do your job," Johnson advised Lestrade. "And be careful. Don't take any unnecessary risks. Beals will leave you alone as long as you don't do anything that could potentially jeopardize his position as superintendent."

Adams looked skeptical. "And how long, exactly, do you think *that* will take?" he wanted to know. "All that has to happen is for Lestrade to stumble across a few more inspectors doing things they shouldn't and insisting on bringing them to justice. Or him causing problems for some rich, upper class *gentleman* who thinks the police are there to do his bidding, or —"

"I see your point," Johnson cut him off, paling slightly. Shooting a worried glance at Lestrade, he said, "I suppose it's too much to ask for you to try to keep your head down."

Lestrade shrugged. "I don't go looking for trouble," he reminded the other man.

"It finds you easily enough," Johnson snapped back.

Lestrade did not answer. The accusation was simply not one he could deny.

He left the three men and returned to his office. He had case notes to organize, and several reports that still needed to be finished. A stack of cases sat on one corner of his desk waiting to be properly filed.

It was mid-afternoon when Inspector Craddock poked his head into Lestrade's office without knocking. Smirking at the youngest and newest member of their ranks, he stepped inside as if it were *his* office rather than Lestrade's.

Craddock was a tall and muscular man with a thick neck, thin brown hair, and bright eyes. His face was entirely unpleasant to look at, partially due to a number of scars that were likely the result of some childhood illness, but mostly due to the way he seemed to look down on every single person that came across his path. Lestrade, younger than most of the inspectors and only recently promoted, was no exception.

The man looked around the room, making a face as if he had judged Lestrade's office and found it lacking. The shorter inspector ignored the reaction, waiting instead for Craddock to reveal whatever it was that had brought him here. After a long moment, the older man turned his attention to Lestrade himself.

"There's been a murder down Ratcliffe Highway," he said. "No one else wants it, which means it falls to the rookie."

Lestrade thought for a moment. "That's on the East End, isn't it?" he asked. Craddock snorted.

"That's why nobody wants it. Off you get."

Lestrade knew a dismissal when he heard one. He also knew better than to argue. Nothing to gain by refusing, and he had no reason to refuse anyway. He had nothing against going; his only issue was with the man currently standing in his office. Craddock clearly did not care what happened to the woman who had been murdered, or he would not be sending Lestrade to deal with it.

The younger inspector grabbed his coat as he left, pausing in the hallway and resisting the urge to sigh as he waited for the other man to step outside so he could close the door. After a moment, Craddock followed, grinning as if he had won a victory against Lestrade.

If he had, Lestrade had no idea what battle he had just lost. Shrugging the thought off, he left Scotland Yard and headed toward London's East End, shoving his hands in his pockets and ignoring the wind that seemed to have picked up right as he reached the street.

Two

A constable stood guard at the door to a set of rooms on Ratcliffe Highway, waiting for the arrival of an inspector from Scotland Yard as patiently as he knew how. He frowned as a man in a dark blue suit caught his eye, mentally preparing himself for a verbal lashing as it became obvious the man was headed his way. The upper class never appreciated being told what to do by the likes of a mere *constable*. Nonetheless, he was determined to do his job. No one was to go in or out until a police inspector had seen to the room.

As it turned out, he need not have worried.

"Inspector Lestrade." The man introducing himself looked barely older than the constable he addressed. Maybe that was why he dressed so well, to offset his obvious youth.

Taking a second look, the other man reconsidered. Without the suit, Inspector Lestrade would have fit right in with some of the lower members of society passing by on the street. Appearances weren't everything, so they said, but Inspector Lestrade did not look entirely trustworthy even dressed as he currently was.

"Constable Mullins, sir." Mullins knew better than to risk the ire of a young inspector who very likely was still trying to prove himself. "The body is inside, Inspector. Mrs. Lowell, the landlady, found it when she went in to demand the rent this morning – apparently the victim hadn't paid for the month, and promised she'd have it today. Mrs. Lowell is in the kitchen on the first floor; she said she had work to do, but you could find her there if you had any questions."

Lestrade looked back over his shoulder toward the stairs. "Any other witnesses?"

The constable simply shook his head. "Mrs. Lowell said no one came when *she* screamed. It's that kind of place, Inspector. If anybody heard anything last night, they won't admit to it."

"Thank you, Constable." Lestrade frowned as the man stepped aside to allow him entrance into the set of rooms.

The first room was bare of furniture except for a badly worn rug that might once have been brown, and a couple of rough wooden chairs. Chipped and badly cracked plates and a few cups were stacked carefully in one corner of the room. Lestrade counted: three plates, three cups. And an odd collection of eating utensils. More than one person lived there.

Lestrade crossed the room and paused in the doorway between it and the next. Here was the victim, sprawled out on the bed, her blood staining the sheets reddish-brown as it began to dry. Lestrade looked around.

The closet hung open, revealing very little in the way of clothing. A battered vanity took up one corner of the room, its mirror cracked. The drawer hung half open, its contents spilled. A brush, a comb, and a hairpin polished so brightly it shone lay strewn about. A chair had been overturned on the floor.

Lestrade approached the bed and turned to examine the woman. Her dark brown hair was sticky with blood; light blue eyes stared unseeingly at the ceiling. Slender and dainty, with small hands and small feet, the woman had been pretty before her death.

Now arms, face, and torso were bruised. Hands were bloodied, nails torn. The victim's face was as every bit as battered as her vanity; the rest of her body matched.

Lestrade examined the room again, more thoroughly this time. He found the remains of a necklace on the far side of the room, flashy yet cheap beads scattered across the floor. Carefully he picked up the string that still held some of the beads, and then began gathering the rest. Reaching the edge of the bed, where the last few had rolled, Lestrade thought he heard a sound and paused.

Kneeling, he reached out with the hand that was not occupied with the broken strand of jewelry and grasped part of the blanket where it had slid partially off the bed to touch the floor. Lifting it he found himself staring at two small faces. Pale and dirty, they stared back at him with wide eyes.

Lestrade momentarily forgot how to breathe. It was likely the only thing that kept him from spooking the children. When he did remember, he forced himself to take a long, slow breath.

The oldest of the children could not have been more than seven. She eyed Lestrade warily, waiting for him to make the first move, while her brother simply stared at him with huge eyes. Lestrade, still hardly daring to move, thought fast.

"I'm Giles," he said, keeping his voice low, hating himself for not coming up with anything better.

The boy looked to be about three years old. He stuck his thumb in his mouth and looked at his sister. She still watched Lestrade, distrust plainly written in her eyes.

The inspector tried again.

"Are you hungry?" The boy's eyes lit up, and the girl bit her lip. Defiantly, she glared at Lestrade.

"What do *you* care?" she demanded, ready to duck further back into her hiding place if she needed to.

Lestrade looked at the boy, then back at her. Then he shrugged. "I've been hungry. I know what it feels like."

"We haven't got any food," the girl told him. "The landlady won't give us none because she says mama owes her money."

Lestrade considered this. "Maybe I can talk to her," he suggested. The girl shook her head.

"Not unless you got money," she told him. She clearly did not believe that the landlady was going to give them anything to eat, or that Lestrade would be able to do anything to change her mind.

"All right," Lestrade gave in. "But I know someone outside who might be able to help. We can talk to him."

The girl looked skeptical. "Mama said stay under the bed and don't come out." The girl's eyes watered. She closed them and shook her head angrily. When she looked at Lestrade again there was accusation in her gaze.

Lestrade thought for a moment. "If I pick you up, and carry you out," he told her, "then you don't really have a choice. I'm too big for the two of you to fight me."

"You'd have to hold us tight, so we couldn't see to fight you," she said, glancing at her brother meaningfully. The girl was smart, for all that she was only seven.

Lestrade reached for the little boy first, ignoring dirt and snot and who knew what else as he scooped him up into one arm. "Eyes closed," he ordered, pressing the boy's face against his jacket, hoping it would block out the sight.

"Eyes closed, William," the girl echoed sternly. She crawled out from under the bed by herself, but reluctantly allowed Lestrade to take her in his other arm.

"You too," he said gently. "Eyes closed." He was relieved when the girl obeyed.

Constable Mullins stared as the inspector emerged from the room with two children in tow, a little boy and little girl, one in each arm. The girl's eyes were squeezed tightly shut; the boy's likely filthy face was shoved into Lestrade's shoulder.

Lestrade met the constable's gaze evenly. Looking down at the children he carried, he said, "You can open your eyes now." Setting the girl down gently, he reached into his pocket and pulled out his wallet. Both children watched with interest, but Lestrade seemed not to notice as he addressed the constable.

"There's a street vendor on the corner," Lestrade told him. "The children likely haven't eaten since yesterday. Try to get more than just bread, if you can."

Mullins nodded and excused himself, making a note to warn the other constables in the area about the new inspector who shelled out money to feed orphans from Ratcliffe Highway. It was only a matter of time before the man ended up mugged or worse, and his wallet ended up in the hands of some street urchin.

He found the vendor, and managed to get a couple of meat pies. On impulse, he bought some tea as well. He had seen the body earlier, when he had first come upon the scene, and figured the inspector would probably appreciate the gesture.

Lestrade and the children waited outside when he returned, the little ones seated on the steps leading up to the building where their mother had died. They stared at Mullins as he approached, taking in the results of his expedition with wide eyes.

Mullins offered the pies to Lestrade, who had pulled a handkerchief from one pocket and spread it across the little boy's lap as if to protect his ragged clothing from the food. Lestrade then turned to the constable expectantly; belatedly he realized the man wanted him to give up his own handkerchief to the girl.

He did, albeit grudgingly. The girl giggled and brushed dirty hands across the white cloth as if to straighten it. Lestrade then accepted the meat pies and began portioning them out to the children.

"Nobody's going to steal it," he said mildly as the girl took a huge bite. "And there's plenty here for both of you." The girl slowed down only slightly, but Lestrade did not seem concerned.

Mullins offered up the tea. Lestrade eyed it critically for a moment, but eventually accepted. Taking a sip, he winced. The constable figured the man had never had the East End's version of tea, and wondered whether Lestrade would finish it, or let it go to waste.

He caught the other man watching him and offered a rueful grin. "I'd forgotten," he admitted, taking another sip. Mullins was impressed in spite of himself.

"I need to talk to the landlady," Lestrade said, turning his gaze back on the two children. "Will you keep an eye on them while I do? I need to find out if they have any relatives they can go to." The inspector sounded almost reluctant; Mullins figured he knew the chances of finding someone to take them in were small. Lestrade glanced towards the girl, who had finished her food and was eyeing her brother's speculatively. "Stay here with Constable Mullins while I talk to the landlady, and we'll see if they have any eels when I get back."

The girl's eyes lit up. "Yes, sir!"

Lestrade had made a friend, of sorts. Hunger could be a powerful motivator, of that he was well aware. Back inside, Lestrade made his way to the back of the building, following the smell of what threatened to be some sort of soup to the kitchen. There he found the landlady, or so he guessed: a sharp, wizened woman with gray hair and cool, calculating eyes.

"Inspector Lestrade," he introduced himself. Mrs. Lowell did not stop her work, but he had not expected her to. "I need to ask you some questions."

"She was two weeks late with the rent." The woman griped. "Always late. Always promising she'd pay me in full next time."

"Do you know the woman's name?" Lestrade asked, reaching for his notebook and pencil.

"Alice. Gardener," the woman replied. "Wasn't married. Had two children, a boy and girl. My boy took an interest in her when she first moved in, before we realized what kind of girl she was. Not that he wasn't still polite, mind you. I raised him up as well as I could after his father died. My Danny's a good boy; he knew better than to go around getting mixed up with her sort." She paused, turning to check on the soup before continuing.

"She used to go out about once a week and stay out all night. Then she'd come back the next morning and pay the rent in full, if anything was still owed. Leave the children at home, of course, to fend for themselves overnight. Over the last couple months she started having visitors here instead. Or maybe it was just the one. I stayed out of it; the less I know, the less the police can hold against me if something happens."

"Do you know anything about her visitors?" Lestrade asked without looking up from his writing. "Height? Age? Hair color? What kind of clothes they wore? Anything would help."

The woman shook her head. "Taller than you, but most men probably are, aren't they?" She cackled. Lestrade ignored the jibe. "Always came after dark. She was always at the door to meet him, so I never had to let him in."

"And did you hear anything last night?" Lestrade wanted to know. "Anything you might have told yourself was just your imagination, or none of your business anyway?"

The landlady looked him over critically. "I heard all kinds of things last night. Nothing that will be of any help to you. Just the usual sounds."

"What about the children?"

"I didn't know they were in there with her, if that's what you're asking." The woman snapped. "I wouldn't leave those monsters in that room with her like that. Even I'm not that heartless."

Lestrade frowned at his notebook. "What about family?" he asked. "Did Miss Gardener have any relatives that you know of? Someone who can take the children?"

The woman shook her head. "No one that I know of," she told him. "That woman was all alone in this world, except for those two children and whatever visitors she had in the night."

Both children were waiting obediently – and quietly – for Lestrade when he returned, but only because Constable Mullins had threatened to tell the inspector that they hated eels and not to give them any if they didn't behave. He felt only a little guilty for threatening to take food from them; from what he had seen of the man so far he doubted Lestrade would go along with it.

"Eels?" the girl asked as soon as she saw him, grinning up at him as if they had known each other all their lives.

Lestrade smiled down at her. "Almost. I need to ask you some questions first." The smile disappeared. "Some serious questions."

The girl nodded, growing serious as well. "William didn't see nothing. He don't know nothing." She said fiercely, putting a protective arm around her brother.

"I understand." This time the man's smile was sad. "Did *you* see anything?"

The girl shook her head. "I heard her crying, though. She kept askin' him to stop. Said he was hurting her. I could hear him hittin' her. And he broke her necklace. The one he gave her. He said she was a liar. And a-a-" the girl swallowed. "I'm not supposed to say that word."

"It's all right, you know," Lestrade assured her, "if you're telling me what happened. It might help to find the person who did this."

The girl nodded. "He called her a *whore,*" she said, nearly whispering the last word.

"Do you know who he was?" Lestrade asked her carefully. "Have you seen him before?"

The girl shook her head again. "We wasn't allowed. Mama didn't like us being around, so we had to leave when he was coming over. Once they was in the bedroom, though, we could stay in the front room until it was time for him to leave."

Lestrade finished writing in his notebook and looked up. "Thank you," he told her. "That does help. One more thing. Do you know if your mother had any family? Brothers, sisters, parents, maybe?"

"No, we don't got any family." The girl told him. "Just Mama." She sniffed, her eyes filling with tears. "Not even that, now."

Catching his sister's sudden change in mood, the little boy whimpered. Mullins fully expected the two to dissolve in tears within the next few minutes, if the inspector didn't do something soon.

Lestrade shifted uncomfortably and reached for his wallet again. "I did say something about eels, didn't I?" His soft inquiry was met with less than enthusiastic nods, but he sent the constable off again anyway.

"I'm sorry," Lestrade told the girl, tucking his hands into his pockets. After a long moment of indecision he continued. "I lost my mother when I was about William's age."

The confession made the girl look up at him. "Lucky I had an older sister to look after me."

She straightened, and put an arm around her brother. For a moment they sat in silence as the child tried to regain her composure. When at last she seemed somewhat in control, Lestrade ventured a question.

"I know your brother's name is William, but what's yours?"

The girl attempted a wobbly smile as she replied, "Rose. Like the flower. Mama always says – said – that I was beautiful like a rose, but I could be prickly like one too." She thought for a moment. "You have a sister too? That used to look after you?" Lestrade nodded. "What's her name?"

"Kristina. She's still looking after me, if you ask her."

Mullens returned then, with the promised eels, and further talk was ignored in favor of paying attention to this second meal. The eels quickly disappeared into the mouths of the two hungry children.

Lestrade watched them silently, but the constable figured the man was weighing his options. He obviously couldn't leave the children to fend for themselves, and hardly seemed the type of person to so much as consider it anyway.

He likely had gotten little help from the landlady in identifying any other family the two might go to. Experience suggested that the murdered woman had no family to go to anyway, if she had been here, living on her own with two children.

Orphanages, often overcrowded, were not much more appealing an option than the street itself. Disease often ran rampant in the places, food was scarce, and beatings were commonplace. The two children might not even be accepted by an orphanage-overcrowding also meant there might not be anywhere to put them.

Workhouses were little better. The work was grueling, frequently dangerous, and the food and shelter received in return could hardly be considered an equal trade. The workhouses were a last resort for most – many preferred to take their chances on the streets.

Mullens had no idea what the inspector planned on doing with the two children, but he did not envy the man his job. Neither the decision regarding what to do with the children nor finding the person responsible for the murder of this woman promised to be simple tasks.

Three

"Do you and your brother have anything you want to take with you?" Lestrade asked. The girl stared up at him in response, horror shining in her eyes.

"What are you going to do with us?" her voice came out in a whisper, nearly inaudible to either man. Mullins had to lean closer to hear her.

Lestrade raised an eyebrow at the child. "I can't leave the two of you here, you know that."

"Why not?" Rose wanted to know. "It's better than the orphanage."

"Mrs. Lowell is *not* going to let you stay," Lestrade pointed out reasonably, and the constable with him felt sorry for inspector and child. It was a difficult conversation for both of them, unless he was greatly mistaken. "You'll end up on the streets, and she'll keep anything that once belonged to you or your mother. You'll be left with nothing but the clothes on your backs."

The girl scowled at him, but for all that she was no more than seven years of age, she knew he was right. Rose had not lived a particularly sheltered life; in fact, her life so far had been anything but, and she knew that all the things he was saying were true. She also recognized that he was, in spite of the harsh reality of his words, doing her a kindness in offering her the opportunity to get anything that was hers or her brother's or their mother's, unless she was greatly mistaken, before the landlady could lay claim to the contents of the room.

For all that he was an adult, and a policeman, this man was trying to help.

"Me and William's things are in the front room," she told Lestrade. "I don't want him going back in there." The inspector nodded.

"He can stay out here with Constable Mullins."

"Mum had a suitcase, but it's in the closet. In the bedroom," Rose told Lestrade as she gathered some clothes for herself and her brother. She also picked up a few wooden blocks and a spinning top and added them carefully to her pile.

Lestrade retrieved the suitcase. Nestled away in the closet, it was unlikely the object held any clues to the identity of the woman's murderer. Careful not to disturb anything else, he returned to the other room to find that Rose had added the dishware to her pile as well. She glared at him defiantly as he set the suitcase down on the floor beside her.

"Those are ours," she told him. Lestrade spared the cracked cups and plates the briefest of looks. Their only possible value was sentimental, though he did not doubt the landlady would try to keep them anyway, if given the chance.

"Anything else?" he asked, and Rose hesitated. The inspector remained still, waiting, while she tried to decide how to answer. After a long moment, the girl looked toward the bedroom door.

"Mama had a comb," she said. "It used to belong to *her* mama, and her mama before that. She loved it *so* much. She always promised she'd give it to me when I was older."

Lestrade *knew* the landlady would most likely be unhappy over that loss. He returned to the bedroom and picked up the comb, examining it more closely. Though somewhat plain looking at a first glance, the comb was not a cheap piece of jewelry. It was made of silver, unless Lestrade was greatly mistaken, with vines twining delicately around tiny flowers and leaves. In the center rested a small but very real opal.

Lestrade frowned at the comb, knowing full well it did not belong here. Not in this dingy apartment, not on Ratcliffe Highway. The girl had claimed it was an heirloom, passed down from mother to daughter over generations, and perhaps it was.

It might have been a gift from her frequent caller, the man Rose thought had killed her mother, though it could just as easily have been stolen. Even if it *were* a family heirloom, there was always the possibility, slight though it was, that he could use it to try to find the murdered woman's family.

He sighed and wrapped it carefully in a handkerchief for safekeeping. He would make some inquiries, and in the meantime the comb would be kept safe from thieving hands. He was not entirely sure that Rose would understand, as young as she was, anything other than that he was keeping the comb, no matter what the reason. There was little enough reason for her to believe she would ever get it back, he supposed. Trust wasn't something freely given; it had to be earned, and he had done little enough so far to deserve it.

Returning to the girl, he knelt down and offered her the wrapped comb, hoping he was not about to make a terrible mistake. "Here you are."

She snatched it from him as if afraid he might change his mind, quickly unwrapping it to make certain the comb was, in fact, actually there. Reassured and a bit surprised, she smiled up at him through tears that had suddenly started running down her face. Throwing herself at him, Rose shoved her face into his jacket and bawled.

Lestrade laid a comforting hand on her shoulder and waited for the girl to cry herself out, ignoring the growing damp spot on his jacket. He did not bother trying to console her; the girl had lost her mother, and nothing he could say would make that any better. The most he could do was sit there and let her cry.

At last her sobs turned to sniffles, and Rose pulled away, red-faced and red-eyed, to look up at him. "You're gonna find him, aren't ya? The man who killed her?"

"I'll do my best," he promised. It was all he could do, really. Steeling himself, he looked down at the comb in her hand. "It's very pretty," he said.

Rose nodded in agreement, her fingers tracing the outline of the stone. "She said never to tell anyone about it. It was our secret. Like a treasure. Nothin' around here is this nice." The girl looked up at him. "This is special, isn't it?"

"Very special," he agreed. Hesitating, he added. "It might be able to help us. Either to find the man that killed her, or to find your mother's family." Rose drew back from him, clutching the comb desperately in her hands. "I promise you would get it back when I'm done."

He let the girl think it through, knowing better than to rush her. "You wouldn't hurt it?" she asked nervously, her own dark eyes staring up into his.

"Not even a little bit."

She worried her bottom lip with her teeth. "You seem like a nice man, Mister," she admitted. "But I've seen a lot of men who started out nice, and then turned mean later." She paused again. "What if you're just pretending to be nice just so you can get the comb for yourself? I bet it's worth a lot of money."

Lestrade did not point out that if he had wanted it for himself, he could have simply kept it and there would have been nothing she could do about it. The argument seemed counterproductive at this point. Instead he reached into his pocket and pulled out his pocket-watch.

"My sister gave this to me, to mark our first year back in London," he said, showing it to her. Wound with a key as was standard, the watch was nothing overly fancy; the case was stainless steel, smooth and unadorned on the outside, with only the engraving *G. Lestrade* on the inside. "I still haven't figured out how she managed to save up enough for it. We came here with nothing but the clothes on our backs, and nearly starved to death that first year before all was said and done, but somehow she managed it. Insisted it was more than just sentimentality; I obviously *needed* one, since I was always coming home late for dinner."

The girl giggled in spite of herself, and reached out carefully for the watch. Lestrade reluctantly let her take it, and she examined it with interest. "Maybe you could hold on to it," he suggested after a moment.

"Like a trade?" The girl was clever. Lestrade again hoped he was not making a mistake. He shrugged.

"More like a promise. That watch means a lot to me, just like your ma's comb means a lot to you. So maybe you could hold on to the watch, just until you get the comb back."

The girl considered the offer for a long moment. "All right," she agreed at last, not without some heaviness. "Just until you're finished with mama's comb." She looked up at him. "Do you really think it'll help find the man that killed her?"

Lestrade knew better than to make promises he was not certain he could keep. "I hope so," he said instead.

Rose offered him the comb, still tucked away in his handkerchief, before secreting his pocket watch safely away on her person. "I'll keep it safe," she promised. "I'll take real good care of it, Mr. Inspector."

"I'll hold you to that," he replied, his tone solemn. "Come on. Let's go."

Talking to the neighbors would have to wait until Lestrade had figured out what to do with the children. Knowing full well it was probably a terrible idea, he took a cab back to Scotland Yard, Rose and her little brother William in tow. The driver balked at taking the two ragged children on until Lestrade politely explained that he was an *inspector* with the Yard, and in the middle of a murder investigation. In the end the children were allowed on, though the driver kept shooting glances at them as if trying to figure out exactly how they were involved. Lestrade did not offer to clear the matter up.

The two children were silent for the duration of the trip, William watching out the window in fascination as the world passed by, Rose more interested in the inside of the cab itself. Lestrade helped them both down when they arrived, then grabbed the suitcase containing their few belongings. Rose took her brother William by the hand then, staring up at the building before them.

"We ain't in trouble, are we?" she asked, her voice suddenly small. Lestrade shook his head.

"Not at all," he promised.

William, who had up until now been both extremely quiet and remarkably well-behaved for both his age and the current situation, sat down heavily on the sidewalk and started crying. Shooting frantic looks around her, his older sister turned and immediately started trying to shush him without success. The boy would not be consoled, and he would not get up from the walk.

They were starting to attract attention. Lestrade took one look around, then another at the exhausted and miserable child before him. Stepping forward, he scooped William up off the ground and planted him firmly on one hip, his arm holding the child in place. Surprised, the boy stopped crying long enough for the inspector to maneuver the suitcase awkwardly into the hand on the same side. Lestrade then reached for Rose, who stood staring at him, with his other hand, and offered the girl a small smile.

"Let's go, shall we?"

Inspector Smith of Scotland Yard had been made previously aware that the newest and youngest addition to their ranks had a soft spot for children while working a case together. The knowledge did nothing, however, to prepare him for the sight of the man somehow managing to carry both a small boy in one arm, suitcase in one hand, while the other led a young girl along beside him.

Smith blinked, then stepped forward automatically to take the suitcase from the younger inspector. "What have you gotten yourself into?" he asked, more curious than worried. Now that the surprise was wearing off, the spectacle was more amusing than anything else, especially considering that Lestrade stood with the child balanced on his hip as if it were the most natural thing in the world.

The other man did not immediately answer, instead shepherding the girl into his office. Once there, he risked setting the boy down on top of his mostly clean desk, clearing the few papers that had accumulated on it in the same motion.

"Someone killed Mama," the girl told Smith, who had followed. Her chin wobbled and her eyes filled with tears, but she did not start crying again. Instead, she turned to Lestrade. "What are you going to do with us?" she wanted to know.

Everything clicked into place. Lestrade did not want to simply drop the children off at an orphanage or workhouse, or even a church. It was understandable; conditions at any one of the aforementioned places could be terrible. Unless they were very lucky, the children could quickly find themselves wishing

Lestrade had simply left them to fend for themselves on the street.

Not, Smith suspected, that the man was capable of that either.

It was obvious Lestrade had no idea what to do with them. Smith was aware enough of the man's personal situation to know that he could not look after them himself until he figured something out; willing or no, the man simply could not afford to. Smith had seen Lestrade's current living situation, and though everything was neat and well cared for, there was no denying that he and his sister had only recently gone from barely surviving to barely making ends meet. What had caused them to struggle financially as they had, Smith did not know, and it would have been incredibly rude to ask.

That did not, however, stop him from wondering.

Smith looked the two over. "Well, I suppose I could take them home with me for the night. Get them cleaned up and a decent meal in their bellies. The missus won't hold that much against me. We can figure out the rest tomorrow."

Something warmed in Lestrade's unnaturally dark eyes. "Thank you," he said, some of the tension bleeding out of his shoulders. "I didn't – I wasn't –"

Smith waved him off. "I was on my way out anyway, and you look like you've got work to do. Have they eaten at all today?"

"The Inspector bought us meat pies and eels!" The girl told him while the man in question refused to meet Smith's eyes.

Smith was not in the least surprised. He smiled down at the girl. "Well, since Mr. Lestrade bought you lunch, young lady, you simply must allow me to treat both you and your brother to dinner. How does that sound?"

The girl looked back to Lestrade for confirmation. The man nodded reassuringly. "All right," she said. "I'm Rose. This is my brother William."

"This is Inspector Smith," Lestrade spoke up, managing to meet the other man's eyes for all of three seconds before looking back at the girl.

"Let me get my coat and hat," Smith told Rose, "and I'll be ready to go."

Stepping out into the hall, Smith made straight for the office across from his own, turning the handle and inviting himself in without waiting for an invitation. Its occupant looked up at him irritably, but waited for him to close the door behind him before speaking.

"What do you want?" he demanded.

"Lestrade caught a murder case," Smith told him. "Two kids just lost their mum."

"Let me guess, he brought them here." Adams retorted with a roll of his eyes. Smith nodded.

"He fed them first." Smith came to the reason for his visit. "Even though he can't afford to." He slapped threepence down on the other man's desk. "Talk to Johnson. Tell him we're taking up a collection to cover the cost. Then do whatever you have to do to bully Lestrade into taking it."

Adams sighed but did not argue, instead digging into his own pocket. "So what happens to the children?" he asked.

"I'm taking them home for the night." Smith told him. "Lestrade can't work and watch them at the same time."

Adams eyed his fellow inspector critically. "And you *can* afford to feed them?" he challenged.

Smith laughed. "My wife makes it her personal mission to feed half the neighborhood's children already. Two more will make little difference." He did not say that it was her way of dealing with the fact that after five years of marriage they still had no children of their own.

Smith left, stopping by to retrieve his hat and coat as promised, then returned to Lestrade's office to collect the children and their things.

"Back already, Inspector?" The greeting was, Mullins was fully aware, not anything near respectful, but he was surprised so see the man again so soon. Not only had he not expected Inspector Lestrade to free himself of the children this quickly, he had not thought the man would be so eager to return to this part of London after having left it so recently. Caught off guard and with the memory of the man feeding a couple of orphans out of his own pocket and then hauling them about as if they were his own still fresh in his mind, the constable momentarily forgot that the higher ranking members of London's police force were rarely men to be crossed, and by the time he remembered, it was already too late.

Lestrade looked the man over as if not entirely certain how to respond, and Mullins hurriedly moved on. "They've taken the body away, Inspector. The landlady is insisting that since the woman was behind on her rent, any property left in the room should go to her as compensation." Mullins hesitated. "I wasn't certain you were finished, so I told her she'd have to wait. Her son's upstairs, lurking by the door to the poor girl's room, waiting for word that you've finished so he can clear it of any valuables."

"Son?" Lestrade asked.

"Danny." Mullins offered.

"I'm finished with the room, but thank you." Lestrade replied. "I hoped to speak with some of the neighbors, see if anyone heard or saw anything."

Again Mullins risked the man's ire. "I doubt you'll get anything, Inspector. They don't much care for the police around here." Lestrade offered him a strange look.

"Nor do they have much reason to," Lestrade pointed out. "Still, I have to try."

"Shall I wait here then, sir?" Mullins offered, "In case it goes poorly?" He winced. He was doing a *terrible* job of keeping his mouth shut this time around.

Lestrade raised an eyebrow at the other man, but did not comment. The constable watched him enter the building, trying to decide what to make of the strange little inspector.

Lestrade's first thought was that he might as well talk to the son and see if he had any information that might be of use in finding the woman's murderer. At the very least, he could eliminate the man as a possible suspect. Unfortunately, the door to the rooms previously rented by the late Miss Gardener were unguarded, the hall empty. Danny Lowell was nowhere to be found.

The family living in the rooms to the right of the murdered woman refused to even open the door. Lestrade could *hear* them moving around on the other side of the wall, but the second he knocked, all went silent. No one answered.

The door to the left opened to reveal a man so drug-addled Lestrade doubted the man would remember him after he was gone. He had nothing to offer other than that the woman next door was very pretty. "It really was too bad," he said, "that she was stuck with those two children. She could have made someone a lovely bride if it wasn't for those brats hanging off her skirts all day."

A woman across the hall opened the door and looked Lestrade over slowly, from his hat to the tip of his shoes, before wordlessly closing the door. He wondered if she had recognized him as a policeman, or had simply decided he was not worth her time. Either way, he would get nothing from her.

It came as little surprise that no one in the building was willing to talk to him, but Lestrade found it frustrating all the same. Most of the people in this part of London were convinced that the police did not actually care about them, other than to blame them for the city's problems, and for the most part, they were right. The only reason *Lestrade* was here was because an older, more experienced inspector had taken one look at the murdered woman's address and decided it wasn't worth his time. A woman had died, and because she lived in the wrong part of London, a member of Scotland Yard had simply written her off.

The inspector sighed inwardly as he returned to the front of the building. He was mildly surprised to note that Constable Mullins still stood guard, and wondered whether it was out of a sense of duty or simply a reluctance to leave while the inspector was still present. Lestrade came to stand beside the other man, wondering how much say the constable had had in his current placement.

"Any luck, sir?" Mullins managed just the right amount of sympathy as the inspector shook his head. He wondered if it were worth making a suggestion, or if the other man would take as him trying to tell an inspector his job. So far Lestrade had seemed a tolerable sort, if a little odd, but it was difficult to tell with inspectors. One wrong word was all it took to set some of them off, especially if they didn't think a lowly constable was being properly respectful of their rank.

Still...

"If you don't mind my saying, sir, you might ask Wilson to put word out, if you're truly interested in finding out who murdered that woman," Mullins suggested. He regretted the offer almost immediately as the other man turned, his dark gaze catching and holding the constable's for far too long. Mullins felt a shiver run down his spine.

"Wilson?" The moment passed. Lestrade pulled out a notebook from his jacket pocket.

"Constable Wilson," Mullins confirmed. "He walks the beat a couple of streets over. Been there twenty years. Prefers it, he says, and he knows just about everyone on his beat. Pickpockets, muggers, thieves – they don't bother him. If anyone saw or heard anything, they'd be more likely to talk to him than anyone else on the force, Inspector."

Lestrade thought for a moment. "Wilson doesn't know *me,* will that make a difference?" he asked.

Mullins shrugged. "He's quick to size a man up," he admitted. "Sees maybe a little more than a body would like, sometimes. If he decides you're trying to help, he'll ask around. Otherwise..."

Lestrade nodded in understanding. "Thank you, Constable," he said, tucking his notebook back in his jacket. "Carry on."

Four

Tall and thin with gray mustache and eyebrows, Wilson looked more like somebody's grandfather than a police constable as he made his way down the street, weaving through the poor folk of the East End as if he were one of them. He nodded to some, waved to others, and swatted tiny hands as they reached for his pockets as if warding them off were simply a game to him. The children, not the least put out by their failure, raced on to find other, more susceptible targets.

Wilson watched them as they found their next victim: a sharply dressed man whose wallet would have been far better off had he stayed clear of parts of London he so obviously did not belong in. The suit was well-made, cut from quality cloth, and *clean*. His shoes, though starting to wear, were the same. The man himself was neat, precise, and cautious; he at least seemed to realize he was out of his depth.

The newcomer caught a small hand as it reached for his pocket without pausing his search of the crowd, impressing Wilson. *Perhaps the man was not so far out of his depth after all.* The child squirmed, and his captor relented, letting him go without a second glance.

Dark eyes found Wilson from across the street, and the constable stilled and waited as the other approached, studying the man all the while.

Eyes that tried to take in everything at once gave the man a nervous, shifty look, and the way he moved, as if prepared for either fight or flight at the slightest provocation, reminded Wilson of the boy he had so recently intercepted. Wariness outlined every movement the stranger made. The combined effect could have been easily mistaken, but Wilson knew better.

He knew a hunted man when he saw one.

"G'day to you, sir," Wilson offered as the man approached. He had to look down a significant distance to meet the man's eyes, and took a moment to guess at his height. *5'6" perhaps. Not more than 5'7".* "What can I do for you?"

"I'm looking for Constable Wilson," the man replied, then caught himself. "My name is Lestrade. I'm an inspector with Scotland Yard, and I was told I might ask him for help regarding a case."

Wilson's eyebrows receded under his helmet. "You've found him. What sort of help, exactly, were you told you might ask for, young man?" he asked, ignoring the man's title. If Lestrade noticed, he did not mention it.

"A woman was murdered on Ratcliffe Highway." Lestrade's voice dropped; Wilson doubted anyone around them could make out the other man's words. "The neighbors won't talk to me, of course. The landlady claims she knows nothing of the woman's business. Constable Mullins suggested you might be willing to ask around. He thought people might talk to you, where they wouldn't give me the time of day." Frustration glowed in the man's eyes only to be quickly banked.

"I could ask," Wilson agreed slowly. "Can't promise anything'll come of it. Folks around here don't really trust the police." Lestrade shifted uncomfortably; the man already knew as much, and to his credit did not seem to blame them.

"I'd appreciate it," Lestrade replied. "Anything you can find out would help."

Wilson idly swatted a hand away from his wallet. Lestrade did not so much as blink. "I'll ask around," he said again, "but don't expect too much."

"Thank you," Lestrade said. Turning, he made his way back through the crowd. Wilson watched him go.

He would talk to Mullins later, find out what had possessed the man to send an inspector, and a fairly fresh one at that, in his direction. The lad must have seen something in the man, to think it worth mentioning Wilson to him.

In the meantime, he would ask around and see if anyone knew anything about Miss Gardner, or about a murder over on Ratcliffe Highway. If he heard anything, he would pay the young inspector a visit and find out whether or not he was serious about finding the woman's killer.

Lestrade relaxed only marginally as he left behind London's East End. A man still had to watch his step – and his pockets – in just about any other part of the city as well. Thieves were less brazen in other parts of London, more cautious and less likely to be seen, which simply meant one had to keep a better look out.

The inspector made his way to Willie's Tavern, knowing the man he actually wanted to speak with would have closed down his shop by this time of day. With any luck, he would have just finished dinner but not had time to drink himself into a stupor yet, and Lestrade would be able to ask him a few questions.

He found Ronald Harris in his usual booth near the back of the tavern, halfway through his meal. Ronald saw him as he approached, smiled, and waved the inspector over.

"Hungry?" Lestrade shook his head. Ronald grinned and waved for a server to bring him a drink instead. "Thirsty?"

"Thank you," Lestrade's polite answer elicited the usual round of mirth from the other man.

Harris grinned at him, not entirely sober, and continued eating while Lestrade considered the drink set before him.

Lestrade had yet to figure out what had caused the other man to approach him that evening four years ago. He had even less of an idea what had made the man decide to sit down and immediately start telling the silent constable everything he could think of about his trade, but Lestrade had sat there for roughly four hours that night listening to the man explain the properties of various metals and how that affected cost and value when it came to jewel craft. If the young man had not uttered a word the entire time, the amiable drunk had taken his silence as an invitation to speak to his heart's content.

Harris had greeted Lestrade like an old friend ever since, always eager to share more about his trade, and Lestrade honestly did not mind that the man never seemed to expect him to say anything in return. On the rare occasion that Lestrade *did* offer the bare minimum of polite conversation, Harris only seemed to view it as a bonus.

"May I ask you a question?" Lestrade ventured before the man could get started on the night's lecture. Harris grinned at him, leaning back in his seat, and picked up his mug.

"Go ahead," he said.

Lestrade offered him the comb that had belonged to the murdered woman. "This is silver, isn't it?"

The other man took the comb and looked it over. "It is. Not plated, either. Silver through and through. Silver-plated items are usually lighter in color. Heavier too, because of the base metal. Silver-plated is more durable, less expensive. This – as old as it is, someone's taken care of it, for it to be in this good of shape."

"I was told it was a family heirloom," Lestrade offered. Harris nodded.

"It's likely," he confirmed. "Pretty little piece. Quite valuable."

"You wouldn't happen to know which family?" Lestrade asked. Harris shook his head.

"I can make some inquiries," he offered. "Was it stolen?"

"Not that I'm aware. A woman was murdered. The comb was either passed down to her through her family, or it was a gift."

"A gentleman's gift," Harris offered. Lestrade shrugged.

"It would be better for any inquiries to be discreet," he admitted. Harris grinned and set his drink aside unfinished.

"Because the woman's family might not want to be associated with her, or because the giver of the gift might be the murderer?" the older man asked, and Lestrade resisted the urge to look away.

"Either is possible," he admitted with some reluctance. "Which is why any questions need to be discreet."

Harris looked uncharacteristically solemn. "Believe it or not, young man, I do know how to keep a secret. I enjoy talking to you, sure enough, and you've been more than obliging over the years, but I'm not the sort to go talking out of turn. You've got nothing to worry about there."

"Thank you," Lestrade reached into his pocket. "One more thing, if you don't mind, Mr. Harris." He held out a handful of the beads from the woman's broken necklace.

"Cheap trinkets," the man asserted immediately. "Bought by women who care more about appearances than actual value, or can't afford anything better."

"What if it was a gift?" Lestrade asked. "From a gentleman caller. Possibly upper class."

"Then he bought it because he thought the woman would think it was pretty." Harris looked thoughtful.

"Could he have bought the comb as well?"

"Wouldn't have bothered." Harris shook his head. "Why give a woman something of actual value when something cheap gets the job done?"

Lestrade considered the question briefly, but lacked the experience to come up with any sort of answer. "Where would someone buy something like this?"

Harris sniffed. "You could find something like this literally anywhere that sells cheap goods," he said. "It's little more than decorative trash. The comb, on the other hand, is a distinct piece, worth tracing." The old jeweler turned his attention back to silver and opal, examining the comb more thoroughly this time.

Lestrade returned the beads to his pocket and watched as the other man lost himself in his work. The inspector nodded as the tavern's owner ambled by on his way to settle a couple of overexcited customers before they could cause any trouble. The man grinned in response but kept moving, preferring overall to keep out of Lestrade's business as much as possible.

Satisfied, Harris returned the comb to the inspector. "I'll let you know if I learn anything," he said.

Lestrade rose from the table. "Thank you, Mr. Harris."

Five

"Lestrade."

The man in question turned around just in time for Adams to shove a crumpled envelope at him. Lestrade fumbled to catch it purely out of reflex, not entirely certain what was being passed on to him. He eyed his fellow inspector warily.

"What is this?"

Adams rolled his eyes at the younger man. "Smith said to take up a collection. Said you shelled out your own money to feed those children yesterday." Lestrade looked away, his face reddening. Adams continued as if unaware of the other man's discomfort. "This should help offset the cost. Don't even think about refusing. You'll offend Smith and Johnson both if you try."

"They're not worried about offending me, though, are they?" Lestrade muttered the question darkly, but the other man still heard it. Adams resisted the urge to laugh; the smaller man clearly felt disadvantaged enough already.

"One day, when you're older and wiser and faced with your own fresh-faced inspector badly in need of looking after, perhaps you'll find it in your heart to forgive them." Adams suggested wryly. "In the meantime, just try not to take it too personally. Smith's heart is quite often bigger than his brain."

With that Adams left, allowing the other man the opportunity to pull himself together.

Lestrade stood still for a moment, debating himself internally, before shoving the envelope into his jacket pocket and making his way back towards his office. He needed to review his notes from the day before and see if there were anything he had overlooked. He also needed to check in with Smith and try to figure out what to do with Miss Gardener's children until they either found someone who could take them or were forced into an alternative.

He had to admit that it was unlikely he would find any family willing to take them in. The woman had been unmarried, living in a squalid apartment with two children born out of wedlock. In Lestrade's experience, a unmarried young woman did not live alone if there were any other options available.

As if summoned by the mere thought of his person, Inspector Smith himself appeared in Lestrade's doorway. The man rapped briskly on the open door as he invited himself inside, offering Lestrade a smile the younger man did not return.

"The missus is insisting that the Gardener children need taken in hand and that she's willing to do so until you find a family member willing to take them." Smith informed the other inspector. Neither man felt the need to comment on the likelihood of Lestrade actually finding anyone. "She insisted on scrubbing both of them down before dinner last night, and she was combing the little girl's curls when I left this morning. I hope that's all right – though if it isn't, I don't know what to tell you, Lestrade. She has her mind pretty well made up on the matter."

"That'll be fine," Lestrade could not quite hide his relief. "Thank you."

Smith shrugged. "By the way, you don't happen to be missing a pocket-watch, do you?" he asked, his tone carefully neutral. Lestrade shrugged.

"It isn't missing."

"Then you know the little girl has it?" Smith asked, curious. Lestrade shrugged again, but did not seem surprised. He also did not elaborate. Smith did not press him. "Let me know if you need anything else from the children."

Lestrade nodded as the older man excused himself. Alone in his office, he pulled out his notes on the case so far and began looking through them, trying to see if he had missed anything.

Inspector Johnson found him still in his office around noon.

"Oh, good. You're still here," the man Lestrade had been paired with his first couple of weeks as an inspector leaned in through the door frame. "Come on. My only suspect in a case I'm working *finally* came out of hiding, and I need someone who can handle himself in case things get nasty."

Lestrade tucked his notebook into his jacket and stood as Johnson explained. "Smith and Adams went out about an hour ago – something about missing jewels – or I'd ask one of them. He's supposed to be making an appearance at that tavern down by Market Street – his brother was shot in the back of the head, and he's my only lead, but the man vanished nearly a week ago, with no one able to offer the slightest suggestion of where he was."

"No one able?" Lestrade repeated, his brow furrowing. Johnson sighed.

"No one able. No one willing. It doesn't really matter which," he admitted. "The point is, someone finally let something slip, and given that the man in question is supposed to be over six foot tall and nearly solid muscle, I'd rather take someone along in case things get violent."

He looked at the shorter man and nearly reconsidered, but Johnson had learned early on that Lestrade was more than capable of handling himself in a fight. No, if the suspect gave them any trouble, he would appreciate having the younger inspector with him.

When he had initially decided to bring Lestrade along, Johnson had somehow managed to forget that while the man *was* more than capable in a fight, he was a terrible conversationalist. It was a fact the more experienced inspector was suddenly reminded of as the two men settled into a corner to wait for his suspect to put in an appearance; Lestrade had not said two words since leaving the Yard, and he did not look at all as if he intended to change that.

Johnson bit back a sigh as he leaned back in his seat. From their current position they could see every angle of the tavern's serving area and both entrances; a third door led to a kitchen, storage rooms, etc. There was no need to keep any sort of watch in the back. If Lewis showed up, it would be as a patron, and they would find him here, in the main room.

"Try not to look so official." Johnson grumbled at Lestrade, who stared back at him without comment. "Or at least, not so uncomfortable."

Lestrade turned his gaze on the drink he had ordered, but made no move to touch it, and Johnson wondered why he had thought it was a good idea to bring the young man along on a stake-out at a tavern; Lestrade did *not* blend in.

"Adjusting to your new position?" Johnson, asked, in a desperate attempt to make the two of them look like two friends out for a drink rather than two policemen looking for someone. Lestrade raised his eyes once again to stare at his companion.

"Yes." At least he had not added, *sir.* Johnson was thankful for that much. He did not offer to elaborate, however, which forced Johnson to cast about for a new topic.

"How's your sister?" he asked, and Lestrade nearly flinched.

"Fine," the other man ground out. Taking a deep breath, he added, "She's made some friends. She says they've been going out walking in the afternoons."

Johnson appreciated the effort. Lestrade was not generally one for small talk, and he did not care to discuss his family at all. The fact that he had given more than a one-word answer at least meant he was trying.

"With some sort of chaperone, I hope." Johnson replied. Lestrade raised an eyebrow at the man, his expression something the other inspector could not quite read.

"One of the ladies' brothers accompanies them, as I understand it." Lestrade offered.

"Have you met him?" Johnson wondered aloud. Lestrade's expression blanked. He was pushing too far, and the younger man did not appreciate it.

"Not yet."

They left it at that. Johnson tried to think of something else to talk about-anything else, really, and kept coming up empty. The awkward silence between them grew.

"Is that him?" Lestrade asked abruptly, his voice low, nodding toward the entrance. Slowly Johnson turned to look.

"It is," he confirmed. Lestrade considered the large man that had just entered the tavern for a moment before turning back to his fellow inspector.

"What was your plan?"

"To talk to him." Johnson replied, eyeing the man as he crossed the room to sit down at the bar. Lewis was a large man, well over six feet tall, and heavily muscled. He also did not look like a man used to being crossed. Johnson wondered briefly if he should have waited and brought more than just Lestrade along for back-up.

Too late now. Johnson stood and crossed the room, coming to stand at the bar beside Lewis. Turning to face the man, the inspector introduced himself.

"Mr. Lewis? I'm Inspector Johnson, with Scotland Yard. We're investigating the death of your brother, and need to ask you a few questions."

Lewis set down his mug and turned to eye the inspector standing before him. "Oh?" he grunted. "Well you can ask. Don't know how much good it'll do."

Johnson cleared his throat. "Actually, we'd like you to come down to the station, where we can talk a little more freely, Mr. Lewis."

The other man chuckled and picked up his drink. "Now that, Inspector, I'm afraid I'm going to have to decline." Johnson sighed.

"It wasn't a request," he insisted. Lewis laughed again.

"Oh, I know." Lewis grinned at him smugly. "You think I killed him, and you want to take me down to Scotland Yard and ask your questions, and then you think you're going to arrest me for it. Unfortunately for you, Inspector, it's just you down here by yourself, in a roomful of people not entirely on good terms with the police. So I'm afraid you're going to have to leave here empty-handed."

Johnson shrugged even as his heart started pounding in his chest. "I was hoping you'd cooperate," he admitted, "and that we'd talk, and maybe find out we were wrong and that someone else killed your brother. But we can always just arrest you right here and now, and take you in for questioning in handcuffs."

Lewis laughed. Standing, he turned to leave only to find his path blocked. Staring down several inches, he took in the smartly dressed and significantly shorter inspector standing before him and snorted, disbelief etched across every inch of his face.

"Get out of my way, boy," he growled. Lestrade met his gaze evenly, though he had to tilt his head back to do so.

Without warning Lewis back-handed the young inspector. Lestrade staggered backwards, nearly tripping over a chair in the process. Lewis laughed again and promptly collapsed as Johnson hit him over the head with his truncheon.

"You all right there, Lestrade?" he asked, reaching for his cuffs. Lestrade straightened, digging in his pockets as he did so. Given the fact that his nose was currently gushing blood, Johnson hoped he was looking for a handkerchief.

Lestrade found the square of white cloth he was looking for and held it to his nose. The man did not look entirely steady. Lewis was strong enough that such a blow could easily have knocked the inspector off his feet.

Lestrade waved him off and headed for the front door, presumably to call for assistance in dealing with Johnson's currently unconscious suspect.

Lestrade's nose had, for the most part, stopped bleeding by the time he returned to Scotland Yard. Crane still stared at him as he reached the man's desk.

"What happened, Lestrade?" Crane ignored the fact that the inspector technically outranked him; they both knew Lestrade was still too new to the position to do anything about it. "Pick a fight with someone bigger than you?" Crane looked thoughtful. "I suppose they're all bigger than you, though, aren't they?" The man broke into in grin, pleased with himself.

Lestrade shrugged as he tried to decide how best to respond. Simply ignoring the man did not seem to be working. "Most of them," he agreed after a moment's thought, choosing to simply answer the question as if he thought Crane actually wanted to know the answer.

Crane rolled his eyes, plainly not amused. "There's a constable waiting for you in your office," he snapped at the other man.

Lestrade left without another word, leaving the desk sergeant to glare at his retreating form as he made his way back to his office.

Constable Wilson waited for him just outside the door, standing at attention. Lestrade wondered briefly how long the man had been standing there, but did not ask. "Come in," he said instead as he opened the door and stepped inside.

Wilson followed him in, coming to stand in front of the man's desk. Lestrade himself took a seat and resisted the urge to wince as he leaned back to study the man. "Can I help you, Constable?" he asked. After a moment's consideration, he added, "Please, have a seat."

"Thank you," Wilson sat down across from Lestrade with a sigh of relief, grateful for the chance to get off his feet, even for a few minutes. "I did some asking around, about the young lady that was murdered. Alice Gardener, you said?" Lestrade nodded absently as he reached for his notebook.

"She kept to herself for the most part, it seemed. Nobody I talked to really had much to offer about the girl herself, but a few of the young urchins that spend most of their time in that area mentioned that she used to go out in the evenings, sometimes, and come back early morning, and that recently she stopped, but that a well-dressed gentleman had started coming around the building about a month or two back, and that he'd come about once a week, after dark, and leave the next morning."

Lestrade looked up. "Well-dressed? How well-dressed?" he asked.

"Not quite the upper class, I don't think. But better off than anyone who lives on Ratcliffe Highway. Middle class, but well-off, one of the boys seemed to think. Came in a cab. Left in the same way."

"Which means he would have had an agreement with the driver," Lestrade said thoughtfully.

"And likely had to pay him extra." Wilson pointed out, in case the young man was not already aware. "It makes them nervous, driving down that way, especially that late."

Lestrade frowned at his notebook. "Anything else?" he wanted to know. Wilson shook his head.

"That's all. It's not much, I know."

"It's more than I had before," Lestrade admitted. "Thank you."

Wilson sighed. "I'll keep an eye out, and let you know if anything else comes up." Both men knew it was unlikely. "Don't get up, Inspector. I'll see myself out."

Lestrade watched him go, then turned his thoughts back to the murder of Miss Gardener. He wondered if it were too soon to expect anything from Mr. Harris. It was unlikely the man would come down to the Yard – the man generally did not care for policemen. Lestrade, oddly enough, seemed to be the exception to the rule. Lestrade would have to go to him, but whether it would be better to go now or to wait until after his business closed the inspector was not entirely certain.

A stack of papers on the corner of the desk caught his eye, and Lestrade decided to wait to talk to Harris. He still had several reports that needed his attention.

Lestrade finished up the most pressing of his reports before leaving his office for the day. This task accomplished, he made his way to Willie's Tavern, hoping to find Harris there and find out if the man had managed to find out anything about the silver comb.

He found Harris in his usual corner. The jeweler smiled and waved Lestrade amiably into the seat across from him. Lestrade obliged.

"I did some asking around, young man," Harris paused to take a drink before continuing. "It turns out one of my colleagues recognized the description of the comb you showed me. He remembered seeing a piece like that a few years back, maybe nine or ten years ago. He was called into appraise a collection, not that particular piece, mind. *That* piece was a heirloom, just as you expected, but my colleague has a special fascination with silver pieces, and knowing as much, they showed it to him. He said it was finely wrought, worth a good bit of money, and a work of art besides." Harris grinned. "Old Merryweather tends to wax eloquent over a good piece of silver. Anyway, he was kind enough to check his records, and was able to find the client, and their current address."

Harris offered Lestrade a scrap of paper. Lestrade took it and glanced at it briefly before tucking it carefully into his jacket pocket with his notebook.

"Thank you," Lestrade said, and Harris waved him off.

"Now, young Lestrade, join me in a drink before you go off back to work." The older man insisted. Lestrade shook his head.

"I have to get home," he admitted. "But I appreciate the offer."

"Well, if you insist." Harris, predictably, was not offended. "Take care, young man."

Lestrade made it home just in time for dinner. His sister Kristina raised an eyebrow at him as he sat down at the table, her expression stern.

"Violet Walker and her brother Joseph will be joining us for dinner Saturday," she told him. "I already told them you'd be there, and that you were looking forward to meeting them."

Lestrade wondered if the woman could have come up with a more outrageous lie, then decided if this were that important to her, he might as well do his best not to embarrass her Saturday evening.

It also occurred to him to wonder *why* it was so important to her, but given the slight pink that suddenly colored her cheeks and the way she fidgeted with her napkin, he was suddenly unsure whether or not to ask, and equally uncertain whether he wanted to know.

"I'll do my best," he assured her, and was only slightly relieved when she relaxed.

By the time they finished eating she had returned almost to her usual self and was intent filling him in on the goings on of their neighbors: one of their neighbor's cats had caught an unusually large rat and left it right outside their door. Lestrade listened with half an ear as he insisted on helping with the dishes, and little by little allowed himself to relax.

Six

The following morning Lestrade found himself at the residence belonging, according to Harris's colleague, to Matthew and Theresa Gardener. The man claimed to have seen the silver comb that had previously belonged to the late Alice Gardener here several years ago, and had confirmed that it was, in fact, a family heirloom.

He knocked on the door and waited, wondering how they would take the news, and whether either parent had heard from their daughter since she had left home.

An older woman bearing a striking resemblance to the murdered woman answered the door. "May I help you?"

"Mrs. Gardener?" he asked, then added. "I'm Inspector Lestrade with Scotland Yard. I'm looking for the parents of Alice Gardener."

The woman frowned, but did not let him in. "What did she do?" she demanded.

"You knew her?" he asked, careful to keep his expression blank and his tone mild. "Forgive me, but were you related to her?"

"Her mother. What happened? Is she in trouble?"

"She's been murdered." Lestrade could think of no better way than to simply say it. He doubted very much that there was a nice way to tell someone that their daughter was dead.

Mrs. Gardener took in a sharp breath. *"Murdered?"* she echoed, drawing herself to her full height as she stared at the man. "How? When?"

"Two nights ago," Lestrade told her. "We're still looking for the person responsible." He paused. "I'd like to ask you a few questions, if possible. Your husband as well."

"You think *I* killed my daughter?" Lestrade shook his head.

"I'd like to ask you some questions about your daughter. Maybe something you know will help us find her killer."

Mrs. Gardener pursed her lips. "I doubt it. We haven't spoken in eight years. Not since she insisted on seeing that *gentleman –*" the sneer on her lips said clearly what she thought of the man, "– against our wishes."

"You and Mr. Gardener objected to her choice of companion?"

"He was up to no good, that one. After one thing, and one thing only." Lestrade felt his cheeks warm.

"Do you remember his name?" he asked, trying to keep his voice even. The woman shook her head.

"David something-or-other. She always called him *Dear David*. I don't know if she ever mentioned his last name."

"Would your husband know?" Lestrade asked.

"I doubt it. He had even less patience for the man than I did."

"And your husband, he hasn't heard from your daughter since she left either?" Lestrade had not conducted a great many interviews standing on the front step, but at least the woman was talking to him. Too many people had shut the door in his face when they found out he was a policeman on this case alone.

"No. He told her when she left not to come back," Mrs. Gardener admitted. "But she was headstrong, and certain she was in *love*, and so she packed her bags and went."

"Did she ever try? To come back?" Lestrade asked. "Maybe she saw the error of her ways and tried to make things right?"

The woman shook her head again. "We never heard from her after that night. She even had the audacity to take my silver comb with her-it was an old family heirloom. She probably sold it a long time ago. I doubt she knew what it was actually worth."

"She stole a comb from you when she left?" Lestrade asked, not caring if the question made Mrs. Gardener wonder about his intelligence. He could read and write, but had had very little formal education, and Lestrade had no doubt that it often showed, even when he did not mean it to. If people chose to think less of him for it, and certainly it had happened more times than Lestrade could count, that was their choice. If he used it to his advantage now and again, Lestrade felt it was only fair.

"Not just a comb. A *silver* comb. An old family heirloom. My mother gave it to me when I came of age, just as her mother gave it to her. It was passed on to Alice on her eighteenth birthday, before all this nonsense."

Lestrade did not ask how it was stealing if the comb had been given to the girl. There was a reason he and his sister had first arrived in London with little more than the clothes on their backs.

Mrs. Gardener sighed. "I would have loved to have been able to give it to Mary. Such a sweet child. Never causes any trouble. Always happy. Always cheerful."

"Mary? Alice's sister?" Lestrade ventured. The woman nodded in reply.

"She'll be eighteen in just a few months. I wish I could have passed it on to her." She shook her head sadly. "Probably long gone. Probably pawned for not even a quarter of its worth." Another sigh.

Conflicted, Lestrade wondered if he ought to say anything. Instead he asked, "Mary wouldn't know anything about this David she was seeing, would she? Or if she was seeing anyone else?"

"I don't think so," Mrs. Gardener replied. "They were never close, even less so after she started seeing *him*."

"Would it be possible to speak with her?" Lestrade asked.

"She's away at school during the week. When she comes home, however, I can ask her if she knows the boy's name. If she does, we'll be sure to let you know."

Lestrade nodded. "Thank you, Mrs. Gardener," he said. He would have to be content with that. For now, at least. Switching tactics, he asked, "If neither you nor your husband kept in contact with her, you wouldn't know of any other relationships she might have been in after she moved out, would you?"

"Absolutely not. I never spoke to her after the day she said she was leaving. Never saw her again." The woman hesitated. "I *hoped* that she came to her senses, that she found a nice young man, got married, and settled down, but clearly that was not the case."

"From what I understand she never married, however, there is another matter I need to speak to you about."

"Oh?" The woman fixed him with a sharp glance, her expression hardening. "And what matter is that?"

"It seems Miss Gardener left two children behind, a boy and a girl," Lestrade told her. "I've been hoping to find family willing to take them in, and you and your husband are the only family I've found."

Mrs. Gardener scowled. "Absolutely not. I'll not have that ungrateful girl's offspring in my house, no knowing who fathered them." She took a deep breath and continued in a calmer, much colder tone of voice. "When Alice left, she knew the consequences of her actions, Mr. Lestrade. I've been as helpful as I can so far, all things considered, and knowing you have a job to do, but when she left she ceased to be family, and I won't take in any so-called children of hers, birthed out of a lifestyle she should have known better than to indulge in."

Lestrade was unfortunately not as surprised as he could have been. He had to try anyway. "They're children, Mrs. Gardener, surely you can't blame them for their mother's actions?"

"Inviting them in would only be inviting trouble," the woman insisted. "Now I'm going to have to ask you to leave, and not to bother us again. Good day, Mr. Lestrade."

With that, she stepped back and closed the door in his face.

For a long moment Lestrade simply stood there. Resisting the urge to shake his head, he turned and stepped down toward the street, trying to figure out what to do next.

He had no idea what to do about the children, and no idea where to look next for the person who had killed Alice Gardener.

Seven

Smith looked up as a knock sounded at his office door.

"Lestrade, come in." He smiled at the other inspector. Fully aware that Lestrade would most likely remain standing unless told otherwise, he waved the man to an empty chair. "Have a seat."

Lestrade obeyed reluctantly. "I found Miss Gardener's parents," he said, not quite meeting the other man's eyes. Smith wondered what it was this time that made him so reluctant, but the tightness in the man's shoulders and around his mouth made it clear that the meeting had not gone the way he had hoped.

"They won't take the children." Smith guessed, and Lestrade's shoulders dropped.

"No," he agreed. Smith sighed.

"I can't say I'm surprised," the man admitted. "If the woman was raising two children on her own, it was probably because she had to. If her parents had been interested in being involved, they would have been. Even if they didn't know, it was probably because she didn't think it was worth trying. Sometimes people are like that," he pointed out, perhaps unnecessarily.

"I know," Lestrade replied. The bitterness in his voice caught the other man by surprise – usually Lestrade was much better at hiding his emotions. Smith chose not to comment on the matter.

"Well, the offer still stands. We're more than willing, so my wife says, to look after them until you find someone who can take them. Maybe their father?"

"If they have the same father," Lestrade pointed out. "If I can find him. If he'll even claim them as his. And if he isn't the one who killed her in the first place."

Smith sighed. "Either way, we'll watch them until you figure something else out."

"Thank you," Lestrade said. There was a weariness in his tone that worried the other man, but Smith knew better than to ask. Lestrade would not thank him for prying into his personal affairs.

"Not at all," Smith countered, offering the man a grin. "Let me know if there's anything else I can do to help, even if it's just to offer a sympathetic ear. You may be a full inspector, but you still haven't been at the job very long. If you need advice – " Smith broke off and winced. "Actually, I might not be the best person to go to for advice, all things considered.

But I'm still happy to listen anyway, if you need to talk through the case."

"I'll keep that in mind," Lestrade said, standing. "I honestly don't know what to do about the children."

"You know what your options are." Smith pointed out. "Short of a miracle, or the grandparents changing their minds, which would probably be a miracle in and of itself, unless I'm greatly mistaken, there's only a few possibilities." Lestrade met his gaze resentfully, and the older inspector shrugged. "Not that there's any rush. And who knows, maybe they'll change their minds after all."

It was unlikely, and both men knew it. Lestrade excused himself after that, and Smith went back to searching his desk for a report he was absolutely certain he had turned in two weeks ago, but that the superintendent insisted had never been filed.

Lestrade wondered, as he sat down at his own desk, if it were worth trying to figure out how many taxi drivers were willing to drive a passenger to Ratcliffe Highway, especially in the evening, and then come back for them the next morning. If the money were good enough, a cab driver might be more likely, but that sort of thing would most certainly be remembered. Whether a man might be willing to make the same trip more than once...

Lestrade scowled at nothing in particular before pushing himself up from his chair. He could try talking to a few taxi drivers, he supposed. Someone might know something, assuming they were willing to talk to a policeman, and assuming they were willing to risk losing a potential customer by talking to him instead of looking for their next fare.

At the very least, maybe he could get some idea of what it would take to convince a cab driver to make the trip to Ratcliffe Highway only to return the following morning.

It was little enough to work with, he admitted to himself as he grabbed his coat, but it was all he had. He would have to make do.

He left his office and turned down the hall, away from the other inspectors' offices. He ignored Crane as he passed the man at his desk, stepping through the doors of Scotland Yard itself and out into the streets of London.

It took him very little time to locate a cab that was not in use; the driver had gotten down from his seat and was whispering conspiratorially with his horse as the two took in the city around him. Lestrade approached man and horse, nodding to the driver.

"Good afternoon, Inspector." The driver grinned at Lestrade while the man was still considering the greeting. "Noticed you tend to walk when you're able, but perhaps you might be needing a ride this time?"

When Lestrade did not immediately answer, the cab driver chuckled. "We met not too long ago, sir, when a gentleman ran out in front of my horse." The man sobered. "Nasty business, that, and Ness here was badly shook up, but I remember you, and so does she. Always remember a kindness, we do, Inspector." The smile returned, if a little more subdued than before. "Now what can we be doing for you today?"

"Just a few questions, if you can spare the time." Clearly more than a bit uncomfortable with the way things were going so far, the inspector still managed to pull himself together. The cabbie – Arthur was his name – nodded agreeably.

"I think I can spare a few minutes, Inspector," he offered. "What sort of questions?"

Inspector Lestrade reached inside his jacket and pulled out a small notebook and pencil. "I know most drivers don't care to work the East End," he said without quite answering Arthur's question. "Especially after certain hours. How hard would it be to find someone to take a fare down near Ratcliffe Highway, at or around nightfall?"

Arthur whistled through his teeth. "I wouldn't do it myself, Inspector," he admitted. "Not for all the gold in the city. But there's a few. Mostly the sort where you'd think twice before trying to skip out on a fare, and there's more than a couple drivers with horses so mean that no one could get near them without bleeding for their trouble. Todd Jefferson, he's got him a horse so mean *he* can't tend to him without getting nipped. Ol' Todd, he'll take you just about anywhere you wanna go, so long as you've got money. He doesn't care where it is, long as he gets paid. George is like that, too, though his horse isn't near as nasty – looks all docile and calm, and usually is, unless she decides you mean trouble for her master."

"Todd Jefferson and George," the inspector paused, but did not look up from his book.

"Sutherland."

"George Sutherland," the other man repeats. "Anyone else come to mind?"

"Gregory Patterson," Arthur offered. "Maybe Charlie O'Keefe."

"Anyone else?" Inspector Lestrade asked, finally looking up from the notebook. Arthur shook his head. "Any idea where to find them?"

"None of them would thank me for giving a policeman their home address," Arthur said frankly. The little inspector did not so much as bat an eye at what amounted, more or less, to an insult to the man's profession. The grudging acknowledgment of the truth in the words reassured the cab driver that he was not making a mistake in offering the man before him information. "Todd and George can usually be found near Fleet Street this time of day, Gregory near Borough Market. Charlie tends to work around Hyde Park."

"Thank you," Inspector Lestrade closed his notebook with an almost audible snap and returned it to his jacket pocket. "I appreciate you taking the time to speak with me."

Lestrade decided to start with Fleet Street, where two of the men he wanted to talk to were most likely to be found. If neither worked out, he would try the market on Southwark Street before heading over to Hyde Park.

Jefferson was no help at all. Once he realized that Lestrade was more interested in talk than in getting a ride somewhere, he clammed up. Urging his horse onward, presumably to look for actual *paying* customers, the man left Lestrade standing by the side of the road, notebook and pencil in hand and absolutely nothing useful in the way of conversation.

Sutherland was not much better. As soon as Lestrade introduced himself, the cab driver gave him a thorough looking over and insisted that not only had he never taken a fare down Ratcliffe Highway in his life, he hadn't been anywhere near the East End for at least three weeks.

Lestrade took a moment, as he was once again left standing in the street with nothing, to consider whether the driver actually knew something, or had simply decided that if a policeman were asking questions about *any* part of London, he wanted no part of whatever trouble said policeman might very possibly be getting him into.

For now, he would let it go, though he fixed the man's face and his horse in his mind, in case the other two names on his list also proved to be less than helpful, and he needed to find Sutherland again.

Lestrade turned his attention to the next name on his list, Gregory Patterson, and began to make his way to the market.

Patterson did not seem to care that Lestrade was a policeman, or that he was more interested in talk than in getting a cab. He also did not seem worried that the questions Lestrade was asking suggested that some sort of crime had taken place, even if Lestrade himself had said nothing to indicate what sort of crime he was looking into.

Patterson grinned at Lestrade, scratched his head, and slapped his horse with more fondness than force. "Sure, we go down that way, when someone asks it. No need to worry, not with Mistress Mary here. Folks foolish enough to cross her once generally ain't foolish enough to do so a second time, and word gets around, especially when looking for trouble with her is liable to cost one a finger."

Patterson chuckled and patted the mare once more. Mistress Mary, as Lestrade had to assume was the animal's name, flickered her eyes back toward her master, but otherwise did not seem to mind either him or the young policeman with him. To all appearances she was indeed a calm, gentle creature, though Lestrade had had enough experience with horses himself that something in the way she held herself gave him pause, just as something in the way her eyes flickered back to him as her master turned away from her made him wary.

"Charge a bit more, though, for the *inconvenience,* if you understand my meaning, Inspector. Can't have people thinking it's a stroll through the park, heading down that way. Even with Mistress Mary here, a man's got to watch his step. And near sundown, like you're asking, cost even more. The missus doesn't like it when I'm late for dinner. 'Better be worth it,' she always says, 'or you can go out and sleep with that wretched animal you're so fond of.' She and Mistress Mary have never really gotten on, but even Ellie'll admit that a man has to make a living."

"What if someone asked you to come back in the morning?" Lestrade asked.

"Have to make it worth the trouble, especially if we're talking early enough to have him back in his own neighborhood before people start to talk. Have to pay ahead of time, too. Wouldn't risk going through all that trouble just to find it was some sort of joke, or he'd gotten robbed or murdered while there. You understand, of course, Inspector."

Lestrade continued writing, not daring to look up as he asked, "And have you done this? Taken a fare down in the evening, dropped someone off, and came back for them in the morning?"

He felt Patterson's eyes on him and looked up, meeting the other man's suddenly solemn gaze evenly.

"Looking for someone specific, Inspector?" There was no way to tell what the cab driver was thinking, or how he felt about the possibility. No way to tell whether or not he would help Lestrade, if it turned out he was, in fact, looking for someone.

"I am," he agreed. "I don't know who it is, *specifically,* but it's a man known to take a cab to Ratcliffe Highway, stay all night, and then leave the next morning, also by cab. He may know something, or have seen something, that could help with a case I'm working."

Patterson eyed him strangely. "A *case?* On *Ratcliffe Highway.*"

Lestrade nodded, but did not intend to elaborate unless he absolutely had to. Patterson let out a low whistle and shook his head.

"And this person you're looking for, he does this often?"

"He's done it at least a few times. Might have been becoming a habit." Lestrade did not like to speculate, but it had been clear enough, when talking to the poor girl's landlady, that the man had stopped by more than once. It had been equally clear that the woman had expected it to continue, had Alice Gardener not been murdered.

"Might talk to Charlie," Patterson muttered, then, more clearly, "Charlie O'Keefe. He was talking about stumbling into a bit of luck. A 'regular' fare, he said, that paid good money, even if he was a bit daft."

"Charlie O'Keefe," Lestrade repeated. "And I can find him around Hyde Park?"

"Thereabouts, most afternoons." Patterson agreed. "Getting a bit late in the day to find him there today, though. He's up before dawn, most days, and home in time to help with dinner; he and the missus take care of her aging father. He tries to make it home in time to take a turn with the old man, for all the good it does him."

"Tomorrow then," Lestrade said with a stab of reluctance. "Thank you, you've been very helpful."

"Good luck, Inspector," the man said. His expression said plainly that he felt Lestrade would certainly need it.

Eight

Lestrade went home. Tomorrow afternoon he would try to talk to Charlie O'Keefe. There was little else he could do today short of going over his notes on the case once more, though if he were being completely honest with himself, he knew he would most likely end up pouring over the pages in his notebook yet again before the day was over.

His sister often said he had trouble setting his work aside at the end of the day, and he had to admit she was right. The murdered woman's battered face still haunted him over dinner – as it had since he had first started working this case. The information he had gathered refused to stay contained within his notebook; his mind insisted on reviewing the facts almost without his permission, each page in his notebook, each written statement echoing clearly in his mind. He almost did not need to go through his notes any more.

Or perhaps it was the number of times he had gone through it that was to blame. Searching through his own admittedly crude version of short-hand whenever he had a spare moment, as if he had missed something, and one more search would reveal the guilty party when it had failed to do so before, and then he could find the person responsible.

It was foolish, he knew, but he couldn't quite help it.

Lestrade looked up and realized Kristina had said something and was, for once, waiting for a reply.

She shook her head in an exasperation that was only partially put-on, but still held enough fondness in the action to take away most of the sting.

"Sorry," he said.

Kristina smiled and waved a hand dismissively. "I'm very quickly learning that you can't help it, Giles." There was no judgment in the statement this time, but Lestrade felt himself flush anyway.

"I said, maybe you need a *hobby,*" she clarified. "Something to obsess over when you're at home that *isn't* work."

Lestrade did not argue with her choice of words, though he did snort at the suggestion itself. It was rude of him to do so, but in his mind hobbies had always been the privilege of the wealthy, and she knew that, if she knew him at all.

"It doesn't have to be an expensive hobby," she protested, proving that she did, in fact, know him fairly well. "Just something to get your mind off work while you're supposed to be resting."

Lestrade decided to humor her. "What sort of hobby?" he asked.

His sister huffed. "Something you enjoy. Or think you might enjoy. I don't know. Something other than just work and then coming home to eat and then work some more."

"Such as?" Lestrade was trying to be patient, but the conversation was putting him on edge. He wasn't sure he needed more than work and a place to come home to at the end of the day. Stability, he supposed, but work provided that, after a fashion. Certainly with his recent promotion they were doing better than they had been.

A safe place to come home to, food to eat, clothes to wear, and a place to sleep at night. Lestrade wasn't really sure he needed anything more. At least, he couldn't think of anything more, except possibly to figure out who had cut short the life of a certain single mother who had been living over on the east side of London.

He figured such an observation would serve only to prove his sister's point, at least as far as she was concerned, so he didn't bother saying any of it aloud.

Kristina shot him a look, as if she knew what he was thinking anyway. She apparently felt she had said enough on the matter, however, because she moved on to a different topic entirely.

"Don't forget Saturday."

Lestrade didn't *think* he had forgotten, but the abrupt change in conversation threw him. His mind scrambled frantically to catch up, but before it could, she shook her head.

"We have company coming." There was just a hint of exasperation behind the words.

"I know. Joseph Walker and his sister. I didn't forget," he almost allowed himself to grumble, but the sudden relief in her eyes gave him pause.

"You'll be there? *On time?*"

"Yes." He didn't promise. He hadn't been an inspector long, but he already knew better than that. His sister did as well. She flashed a bright smile at him anyway, and once again Lestrade found himself wondering exactly what this dinner meant to her, because it clearly meant *something*.

It might just have been that it was the first time she'd actually had a friend over for dinner, at least with him there, which might in turn mean that she was finally starting to feel at home here, in this small set of rooms in the middle of London.

Lestrade wasn't sure. Truthfully, he still hadn't figured out what home was supposed to feel like.

Lestrade turned his thoughts back to his sister with effort, watching the way her cheeks reddened uncharacteristically, and how she was suddenly very busy with her plate, and was forced to admit, if only to himself, that there might be more to dinner on Saturday than Kristina simply having a friend and her chaperone over to visit.

The rest of the meal passed, for the most part, in silence, though not an uncomfortable one. Once finished, Kristina stood to clear the table, and Lestrade moved automatically to help her. This task complete, they started on dishes, Kristina washing and rinsing the dishes while her brother dried and put them away.

Once they had cleaned up, they found themselves back at the table, each with a needle in hand, a basket of mending between them. The evening passed in companionable quiet, for Lestrade never had been much of a talker, and Kristina always seemed to know without him having to say it when her brother was near his limit.

There was a brief moment of confusion for Lestrade when he reached into the basket and pulled out a shirt that was most certainly too small to be Kristina's. "What's this?" he asked.

His sister shook her head but didn't quite laugh. "I've been taking on some of the neighbors' mending. Mrs. Brown doesn't have the time to do her own, not with four little ones to manage, so I offered, and Mr. Andrews down the hall overheard and admitted to being hopeless with a needle. It's not much, but I've been able to put aside a little bit this month, just in case."

Lestrade simply nodded and started on the shirt.

Lestrade spent the next morning in his office, catching up on paperwork that never seemed to *stay* caught up in spite of his best efforts. Smith dropped in briefly around mid-morning with a report on how the Gardener children were doing under his wife's care, reminding Lestrade that he also needed to figure out what to do about *them* without explicitly saying as much.

He was no closer to figuring that out than he had been the day he brought them to the Yard with him. He was well aware of his options, aware of how awful they were, and still did not have an answer. Probably he needed to just make a decision and get on with it, but something held him back, though he had no idea what.

It certainly wasn't some misguided hope that the murdered girl's parents would change their minds. Lestrade wasn't foolish enough to expect that. He knew full well that there would be no reconciliation between the children and their grandparents, and some small part of him wondered if it were better that way.

Still, it would most likely have been better than any of their other options.

Smith, mercifully, didn't ask if Lestrade had made any progress in finding a place for the children. He simply reported that his wife had the children well in hand, offered a sympathetic smile Lestrade didn't know what to do with, and assured the younger inspector that they were in no hurry to be free of the little ones before excusing himself.

Lestrade let out a breath he didn't know he was holding when the man left before turning his attention back to the papers on his desk.

Lestrade found Charlie O'Keefe in the first taxi cab he found, waiting across the street from the entrance to Hyde Park.

The man was reluctant to talk to him at first, especially when Lestrade mentioned Ratcliffe Highway.

"Look, Inspector, I haven't done nothing that's against the law, and that's a fact," the man insisted. "I just take people where they want to go, and mind my own business when it comes to why. Nothing illegal about that."

Lestrade resisted the urge to sigh. "I'm not looking to cause trouble for you," he said bluntly. "A girl was murdered. I'm looking for the person responsible. The landlady said there was a man who would stay the night, and I'm trying to track him down. Maybe he did it, maybe not. But either way, it's not likely he'll be going back that way again."

O'Keefe glared at him for a moment, then his shoulders slumped. "I suppose you're right," he admitted. "If she's dead there's no reason for him to go back. What is it you want to know?"

"Tell me about your overnight fare. The one you dropped off in the evening and came back for the next morning."

O'Keefe looked at Lestrade for a moment, startled, then shook his head. "All right, so a couple of months ago, a man comes up to me here at the park, says he's looking for someone discreet. Tells me he's in love, that he's met a girl and he's going to marry her; he's just got to talk his mother around. That in the meantime, he just *has* to see her. Then he tells me where she lives."

Lestrade, notebook out and pencil already moving, nodded for the other man to continue. After a moment, he did.

"I was hesitant at first, I'll admit. But he was insistent, and asked what I thought was fair – then he offered to *double* it, if I'd pick him up here in the evening, at sunset, and drop him off. Said he'd pay me the same again to pick him up at dawn the next morning, and bring him back. I agreed; it was more money than normally I make in a week, to be honest, Inspector, and it's not like we couldn't use it. Next week he comes back, offers me the same deal. Turned into a weekly thing, and it's sure been a help to me and my wife."

"And this went on for how long?" Lestrade asked. "Two, three months?"

"Two months and a week." O'Keefe confirmed. "I picked him up here at the same time every week, dropped him off, and picked him up at the same time the morning after."

"And did he give you his name?" It would make Lestrade's life that much easier if he had, but if he was worried about the cab driver being discreet, it was highly likely he had not.

The other man shook his head. "Sorry, Inspector."

"Can you describe him for me?"

O'Keefe looked off across the street, thinking. "Might be able to do that much," he admitted. "Let's see. He was fair-haired. Tall. Well-dressed, upper middle class I'd say. Had a mustache and carried a cane, but didn't really use it. Handsome fellow, really. Could have done better than some wretch over on the East End, but that's none of my affair."

Lestrade paused in his writing and looked up. "Was he usually waiting for you? Or did he arrive after you?"

"After," the man admitted.

"And did you notice how he got here?"

"Usually came walking up the street from that direction." O'Keefe gestured. "Never looked particularly out of breath, so he couldn't have been walking far, I'd guess. His clothes were always neat too, never out of place."

"This side of the street?"

"Yes."

"Anything else you can remember about the man?" Lestrade asked, looking up from his notebook.

O'Keefe shook his head. "Nothing else comes to mind, Inspector."

"It's more than I had before," Lestrade admitted, closing his notebook and tucking it into his jacket pocket. "Thank you for your time."

Lestrade left the cabbie and started down the street in the direction the man had pointed, eyes on each building as he passed, looking for anything that might suggest the man he was looking for had stopped by.

By the time Lestrade made it back to Scotland Yard, he had a list of possible places a middle-class young man might have stopped by on his way to meet O'Keefe, but nothing certain. It did seem highly unlikely that the man had walked to Hyde Park from his home, though that still left plenty of possibilities. He could have simply taken a different cab and asked to have been dropped off a few blocks up the street from Hyde Park.

He also could have stopped at one of the businesses along the street and spent a few hours there before meeting the cab driver that evening. There were more than a couple places he could easily have spent the afternoon.

Lestrade shook his head. It was all guesswork, and guessing would get him nowhere. What he needed was solid information, and some way to identify the man who had been at Alice Gardner's the night she died.

He figured he might as well stop by each business along the street and ask if anyone recognized the man he was looking for based on the description the cabbie had given him. It wasn't much to go on, and he was willing to admit as much to himself at least, but it was all he had.

He would go back out first thing tomorrow.

Nine

Smith found Lestrade on his way to his office the next morning.

"Got a minute?" he asked, his voice low. Lestrade turned and looked at him for a moment, expression unreadable, before nodding. Smith led the man into his office.

"It's about Rosie – the girl?" He paused, and Lestrade braced himself as if for bad news. Smith wondered idly if the other man realized he was doing it, but didn't bother asking. A question like that would only make Lestrade *more* wary around him. "She's been upset the last day or two. Crying. Something about a comb. She keeps saying you promised you'd give it back, but..." Smith trailed off as Lestrade reached in his pocket and offered the man something wrapped in a plain, white handkerchief.

Smith unwrapped it, and let out a low whistle. Silver, unless he was mistaken, and worth a pretty penny. "This is hers?" he asked.

"It was her mother's," Lestrade explained. "Family heirloom. Hers now, I guess."

"And she just let you have it? She hasn't shown herself to be a particularly trusting little thing so far."

To his surprise, Lestrade chuckled and shook his head. "You asked if I knew she had my pocket-watch," he said.

"I see." Smith eyed the comb. "I'll make sure she gets this," he said, wondering if the other man trusted him to do just that. "And that you get your watch back, of course."

He had seen the watch, a plain, ordinary looking timepiece, exactly what one might expect of the man standing before him, with the possible exception of the *G. Lestrade* inscribed on the inside in an elegant script that he doubted the man would have chosen for himself. He had noticed, too, that it had been well-cared for.

That watch meant something to Lestrade.

The younger inspector only nodded, however, and excused himself, leaving Smith standing alone in his office.

Lestrade returned to his own office, closing the door behind him. Going to his desk, he took a quick inventory of everything on it – mostly neat stacks of paperwork, some yet to be completed, some needing one last going over for errors in spelling or grammar, and some waiting to be turned in. A dictionary took up the top right-hand corner of the desk. A couple of carefully sharpened pencils rested beside the well-worn book.

Lestrade sat down and reached for a sheet of paper, then for a pencil. Pushing the case of the murdered woman to the back of his mind, at least as much as he was able, he got to work.

He spent the next couple of hours working, filling out forms with painstaking care and consulting the worn dictionary on his desk when needed. There was plenty to do even without trying to find the person responsible for the death of Alice Gardner –relatively new to the job or not, no one was taking it easy on the "new" inspector when it came to handing out assignments. If anything, Lestrade tended to catch the cases that no one else wanted to deal with. Even Johnson had been guilty of passing a few undesirable assignments Lestrade's way, though nothing overly dangerous, and certainly nothing that he thought had even a remote chance of getting Lestrade in trouble with any of the other inspectors – no, anything Johnson passed on tended to be mildly annoying at best, stuff the older inspector didn't have time to deal with – or, if Lestrade were being honest with himself, simply did not want to.

Lestrade honestly could not say that he minded being sent out for the sort of cases that most of the other inspectors considered not worth their time. At least, he did not mind dealing with the cases himself. It was all part of the job, even if it was not particularly exciting.

Not that Lestrade had become a policeman because he had thought it would be exciting. If anything, he *preferred* the smaller, less violent cases, where no one had been hurt, no one had been murdered, and no one had been kidnapped.

No, what bothered Lestrade about the whole affair-or would have, if he let it, was the way the other inspectors dismissed the smaller cases as not worth their time. A drunk disturbing the peace. An argument between two former friends. A young woman with a missing child. A single mother of two murdered in the wrong part of town. The attitude that only certain crimes – certain *people* – deserved their attention, *that* bothered Lestrade.

Not that there was much *he* could do to change their minds. Lestrade could no more change the way his fellow inspectors thought than he could change the way the general public viewed the police force.

That Lestrade could understand. Especially when it came to the poor, and the so-called undesirables of the city. Why should they care what the police have to say, why should they trust anyone from Scotland Yard, when the best they could hope for was to be ignored?

Lestrade did not have an answer, any more than he had a solution.

Lestrade had *not* forgotten that his sister was having company over for dinner; however, the remembering did nothing to save him from the uncomfortable reality of two complete strangers talking and laughing with her in the kitchen when he got home. For a moment he hesitated in the other room, the childish urge to hide hitting him, but the knowledge that Kristina would not only never forgive him, but also in all likelihood come after him, kept him in place.

He took a deep breath and made himself enter the room.

His sister looked up almost immediately, her eyes sparkling in a way that he had not seen since they were both very young. She was still laughing as she waved in his direction, a wordless order to not only come in and be civil, but to join in on the conversation; by now Lestrade could tell the difference, at least with her.

With no other option available, Lestrade left the safety of the doorway and came to stand next to his sister by the stove. Taking pity on him, the woman offered him the spoon she was using to stir a pot full of some sort of thick stew. Lestrade accepted it with relief and turned his attention to the soup. A gentle nudge against his free arm warned him that he was not going to be able to get out of socializing with her friends.

"This is my brother Giles," Kristina offered, introducing him to their guests. "Giles, this is Violet and her brother, John Walker."

Lestrade didn't miss the slight pause before Kristina offered the man's last name, but since he did not know what to do with the knowledge, he simply refused to acknowledge it. Instead he nodded to both Violet Walker and her brother and went back to stirring the soup.

"Miss Lestrade tells me you're a policeman." Lestrade looked up at that, but Mr. Walker's expression gave away no indication as to how he felt about it. Whether he, like a majority of London, found it distasteful, Lestrade could not tell.

"Detective Inspector," Lestrade clarified, flicking a glance towards his sister in case *she* knew. He got nothing. Kristina was looking at her friend instead of him, and Lestrade could not see her face.

"You were involved in that case with the slave traders?" the other man asked. His sister cleared her throat and shot him a meaningful glance, and he backtracked. "Not exactly polite conversation for the table," he amended with a smile that was just a fraction too wide for Lestrade's comfort. "Or for the womenfolk," he added, receiving a sharp look from both women for his trouble.

Lestrade found it safer not to comment.

"John's a gardener," Kristina said, changing the subject. "You should see his roses, Giles. So many different colors! I didn't know there were so many different kinds."

Mr. Walker smiled and shrugged. "I've always loved plants. We used to live in the country, when we were little. Our parents moved with us into the city – I must have been what, nine years old? I hated it."

"He missed being able to wander the countryside all day," Miss Walker put in, her voice soft as she stared somewhere halfway between Lestrade and his sister. "He'd be up and out the door before sunrise and wouldn't be back till close to dark." She offered a tiny smile. "He also hated school."

Mr. Walker sighed and looked up at the ceiling. "You always were better at reading and writing," he conceded.

"And sitting still," his sister teased gently.

"I'd love to go back someday," Mr. Walker said, smiling again.

"To school?" Kristina, quick as ever, shot at him, startling the man's sister into a laugh that quickly turned into a cough. Mr. Walker himself chuckled.

"Never," he declared. "I meant the country. Get away from the crowded streets and all these people. Do some farming, maybe get some chickens, some cows, a goat or two..."

"Sounds lovely," Kristina said, smiling.

The rest of the evening passed by in much the same manner, with Kristina and Mr. Walker doing most of the talking. Miss Walker seemed content mostly to sit and listen, adding to the conversation only occasionally. Giles himself had very little to offer, but for once his sister did not seem to mind.

He was half expecting her to suggest that he could have been more outgoing as the door closed behind their guests, and she turned back toward him, but instead Kristina grinned.

"Well, that went well," she declared. "Don't worry about the dishes, Giles, I'll clean up."

Giles was not sure exactly *what* had gone so well, but he certainly was not going to ask, not when his sister looked as pleased as she currently did.

He settled for sitting at the kitchen table while she worked, listening with half an ear as she talked about how nice it was to have friends over, and how much she enjoyed Violet and her brother's company at dinner, and how they would have to get together again some time soon.

Ten

"There's a gentleman waiting to see you in your office, Lestrade."

Inspector Adams did not so much as pause as he passed the other man in the hall, leaving Lestrade no other option than to call a hasty "Thank you," over his own shoulder at the older inspector's retreating back and hope that Adams heard him.

The gentleman in question seemed to be just that – a gentleman. His clothes, his posture, the way he reclined in the chair in front of Lestrade's desk and took in the room as if he owned it – everything about him suggested that the man came from money.

He was also fairly young. Lestrade figured the man was in his early twenties, certainly no older than twenty-five at the most. He had blonde hair and a mustache, blue eyes, and a semi-muscular build. He was also only a few inches taller than Lestrade, the inspector noted as the man noticed him and rose to his feet.

"Inspector Lestrade?" the young man asked. When Lestrade nodded, he continued unprompted. "I just heard the news last night, Inspector, and was told you were investigating the case. I can't believe it, Inspector!" He stepped closer to

Lestrade, close enough to reveal dark circles under red-rimmed eyes, as if the man had not only not slept the night before, but had been kept awake by some great personal tragedy. "My Alice – who could have done such a thing?"

"Alice Gardner?" Lestrade asked, stepping farther inside his office and guiding the young man back to his chair." The other man nodded.

"The landlady said she was murdered," he said, sitting back down. "Please, she had to be lying, or maybe it was some sort of joke?"

"I'm afraid not." Lestrade found his own seat behind his desk. "Mister – ?"

"Marcus. My name is Marcus." The young man replied. He looked away for a moment, distraught. "She's dead, then."

"Yes, sir." Lestrade wondered if this conversation ever got easier. "How did you know the deceased, Mister...Mr. Marcus?"

"Please, just Marcus," the man corrected. "We were seeing each other – well, we were in love, to tell you the truth, Inspector. I wanted to marry her. I was trying to talk Mother around. The thought of me marrying below my station was absolutely abhorrent to her, but I had almost gotten her to agree to meeting Alice. I was sure if Mother just had a chance to *meet* her she would see what a wonderful woman she is – sorry, *was*."

"And Alice felt the same way?" Lestrade asked. "In love? Wanting to marry?"

Marcus turned to stare at him. "You think *I* did this? I loved her!"

"I have to ask. Witnesses reported overhearing a quarrel between two people the night she died."

"Of course." Marcus took a deep breath, collecting himself in the process. "Of course. Yes, she loved me too. And she wanted to get married. She was nervous about meeting Mother, but wanted to try; her own parents had disowned her when she was younger. They didn't approve of the man she was seeing at the time. She didn't want me to have to go through the same thing."

"I see," Lestrade nodded, thinking. "Were you aware that she had children out of wedlock – a boy and a girl?"

"I was. I never got to meet them, but I was aware that she had them. To be honest, Inspector, I didn't care. I *loved* Alice. If marrying her meant taking in her children as well, I was willing to do so. She was worth it."

Lestrade nodded and made a few notes in his notebook. "You understand I have to ask where you were the night she died?"

"Of course." The young man shuddered. "I was having dinner with Mother and her friends. It's a regular occurrence. I'll admit that I was trying to charm her, hoping that after she would be in a more reasonable state of mind to discuss Alice."

"And was she?"

"No. It turned into quite the disagreement, I fear. Once Mother gets started she can go on for hours. I believe it was close to one in the morning before we parted – the servants can attest to that. They can also verify that I retired to my room immediately after, and did not come back out until the next morning."

"I'll need to speak with them to make sure," Lestrade said, half expecting some sort of protest.

"Feel free to stop by this afternoon. I'll let them know to expect you." Marcus sighed, "I can't believe she's gone."

"Do you know anyone who might have a grudge against Miss Gardener? A neighbor, perhaps? Maybe another-visitor?"

Marcus laughed outright, and Lestrade felt his cheeks warm slightly. "She stopped seeing anyone else months ago. I told her I loved her, and perhaps it was foolish of me, but I thought she might feel the same way..." He shrugged. "As it turned out, she did. Most of her other *visitors*, as you called them, were happy for her. Alice was that kind of girl. She made friends everywhere she went. People adored her."

Lestrade considered this. "And none of her visitors were jealous, either of you, or of her?"

Marcus shook his head, then paused. "None of her visitors, no. But there was a young man –I think he was actually the landlady's son. I caught him watching her from the hall a few times. He knew I'd caught him too; he'd stand there and scowl at me for a minute before retreating into the kitchen. Alice said he was nice to her when she first moved in, but once she started *seeing* people he stopped talking to her."

Lestrade made a note to talk to the landlady again.

"Anything else you can tell me? Anything that might help us find the person responsible?"

Marcus shook his head. "Nothing, Inspector, but I will certainly let you know if I think of anything else." He paused for a moment before asking, "The children – what happened to them? Are they all right?"

"They're safe." Lestrade assured the man. "We're currently trying to find family willing to take them in, but in the meantime, they are being cared for."

Marcus nodded. "I would offer to take them, but Mother wouldn't stand for it. If we had gotten married, it would be one thing. Now – well, let me just say I hope you find someone. Alice's parents, perhaps – surely they wouldn't punish the children for the perceived sins of their mother." Lestrade did not explain that they had already tried, and failed, to reason with the parents. "I would appreciate you keeping me informed, Inspector. About the children and in your search for dear Alice's murderer."

"I'll share what I can." It was an empty promise, but it seemed to reassure the man. Marcus stood, offered Lestrade his hand as if they weren't from two completely different worlds, and thanked him for his time before excusing himself.

It was not a situation Lestrade often found himself in.

Inspector Smith found him not too much later, still in his office. "Before I forget," he said, offering Lestrade his pocket-watch. "I don't suppose you've had any luck finding anyone to take the children." Lestrade shook his head as he reclaimed his watch.

I found the woman's gentleman-caller," he admitted. "I may have found another lead when it comes to her murderer, but not as far as the children. He insisted *he* couldn't take him because his mother wouldn't approve before I could even ask."

Smith shrugged. "I just thought I'd check in. The missus isn't in any hurry to see them gone, and your job is to find her murderer, not run around London looking for a good home for a couple of orphans."

"I'm aware," Lestrade replied, in a tone that suggested he felt he was every bit as responsible for finding the children a home as he was for finding their mother's murderer.

Smith shook his head. Lestrade was going to have to learn, sooner or later, that there was only so much one man could do.

It did not take Lestrade long to find the house. Marcus had given his address before he left that morning, and Lestrade had recognized the area; the man lived in a fairly wealthy area of London.

He had also been true to his word in letting the servants know to expect him. Lestrade was welcomed in almost immediately and taken to the kitchen where more than one servant was able to verify the man's account of the events that night.

An older woman entered the kitchen just as he was getting ready to leave and introduced herself as Marcus's mother.

"I understand the girl he wanted me to meet was murdered," the woman said. Her expression remained politely disinterested; there was no way to tell what she actually thought about the matter. "I am sorry to hear that. I did not approve of the match, but the girl deserved better, and her death has certainly left my poor son bereft." She shook her head. "It was such a shame-I was just thinking yesterday that surely there would be no harm in agreeing to meet her. After all, it seemed to mean so much to my poor Marcus."

Lestrade nodded along, then asked, "He said you had a disagreement on the matter?"

"Yes," the woman confirmed. "He wanted me to meet her, and at the time I told him there was little point in my doing so as it would not change my mind. He grew frustrated, insisted that I wasn't even giving her a chance. I'm afraid it devolved into quite the shouting match. We were up until roughly one in the morning arguing. He went straight to bed after that; he was quite upset."

Lestrade left the house with a confirmed alibi, but nothing more. According to the household, Marcus had not killed the woman he claimed to love.

Lestrade's next stop was Ratcliffe Highway itself, and he nearly got his pockets picked for his trouble in the process. He could hardly begrudge the urchins that kept swarming around him-they were on the whole thin, ragged, and clearly half-starved. He caught little fingers before they could make their way to his wallet, offered a few stern looks, and moved on.

He found Miss Gardener's former landlady in the kitchen, just as he had the last time they spoke. She eyed him sharply as he entered, but did not pause in slicing vegetables.

"Inspector," she greeted him as if he were an unwelcome guest she could not quite get rid of. "Any luck finding the killer?"

Lestrade shook his head. "We managed to track down her guest, but he has an alibi for the night she was murdered." He eyed the knife the woman currently held as he continued, "The man seems to think your son might have seen something?"

"*My* son?" The woman's eyebrows lifted, and there was a warning in her voice as she asked, "Now why would he think my son would know anything? That woman never so much as gave him the time of day."

"Apparently Miss Gardener mentioned that your son was nice to her when she first moved in," Lestrade offered.

The woman scowled. "We may not have money, Inspector Lestrade, but I raised my son the best I could. I taught him manners, and I taught him to be gentle. If he felt sorry for the girl when she first moved here, he may have had a kind word for her now and again. That doesn't mean he regularly associated with her, and it doesn't make him a suspect."

"Of course not." Lestrade felt it prudent to agree as the woman gestured with the knife in her hands. "But if there's a chance he saw something, I need to speak with him."

"He's not here," the woman sniffed, and went back to chopping vegetables. "He works hard, my boy does. Honest work, too, he does. He won't be back until late this evening."

"What time?" Lestrade asked.

"He usually gets in around eight o'clock," she offered reluctantly. "Sometimes he stops for a drink with the boys, then it's usually closer to nine." She scowled down at her chopping board, knife still busy. "I assume you'll be back; I'll make sure he waits up for you."

Constable Wilson was standing on the corner as Lestrade stepped out into the street. The Inspector turned and went to meet him, wondering if it were simple coincidence that had brought the man here, or if he had come looking for the inspector.

"One of the boys mentioned you were back," the constable greeted him. "Said his friends were making plans. They see you as a challenge, given that no one's managed to pick your pocket yet in spite of the fact that you stick out like a sore thumb around here."

"Is that a warning?" Lestrade asked, eyebrow quirking upwards. Wilson chuckled.

"Something like," he admitted. "Seems a shame to leave you to fend for yourself, especially since Mullins insists you were shelling out your own money to feed a couple of freshly orphaned children." Lestrade shrugged, resisting the urge to look away. "He also seemed to think you were making it your personal mission to find a home for them."

"Couldn't just leave them," Lestrade muttered. Wilson shook his head, but did not disagree.

"Any luck?" he asked.

"One of the other inspectors and his wife are looking after them for now," Lestrade admitted. "We found Miss Gardener's parents, but they wouldn't take them."

"No surprise there," Wilson said. "And the case itself? Any leads?"

"Her gentleman caller has an alibi," Lestrade ventured. Turning to study the man, he asked, "He said there was some tension between the Miss Gardener and the landlady's son. Know anything about him?"

"Who, Danny?" Wilson asked, frowning as he thought. "Works down at the docks. Hangs out with some rough characters. He's the sulky, surly sort. Not particularly friendly. Stays out of trouble, though."

"His mother said he'd be home around eight. That I could speak with him then."

"These streets aren't exactly safe after dark," Wilson cautioned. "Not even for an inspector, and especially not for one so smartly dressed."

Lestrade shrugged. Dangerous or not, he would do whatever he had to in order to find Miss Gardener's killer.

Wilson tilted his head slightly, favoring the younger man with critical eye that made Lestrade distinctly uncomfortable. He had never much cared for being studied, especially not with the intensity Wilson was currently devoting to the process, however, Wilson, while older, did not outrank him.

Lestrade resisted the urge to fidget and met the other man's gaze squarely. For a brief moment, one that felt far longer than the few seconds it actually lasted, the two men stood staring each other down.

Lestrade wondered what the other man saw, but pushed the thought away quickly. There was little point in wasting time on the thought; Wilson would either speak up and say what was on his mind, or he would not. He did not strike Lestrade as the kind of man to be easily persuaded to do one once he had decided on the other.

"I'll see you at eight," the man said solemnly. He turned and walked away while Lestrade was still trying to figure out what had prompted the decision, leaving the slightly baffled inspector staring after him as he made his way down the street.

Eleven

True to his word, Constable Wilson was waiting at the nearby street corner when Lestrade returned to speak with the landlady's son. The other man greeted him with a nod, falling silently into step with Lestrade and adjusting his stride to match the shorter inspector's own.

Wilson stopped as they reached the building itself, coming almost to attention at the bottom of the steps leading up to the front door. Another nod, and he settled into his self-appointed post to await the younger man's return.

Lestrade was not entirely certain he needed a guard, but saw little point in arguing the point, not when he had other things to do. Leaving the constable to stand watch, he stepped up to the door.

He stopped as the sound of two people arguing reached him; judging by the fact that he could hear them from outside, Lestrade suspected they were both standing in the hall on the other side of the door.

There were two voices: one male, one female. Both were angry. Lestrade was almost certain that the female voice belonged to the landlady, but he did not recognize the other. He paused, debating whether to knock and risk interrupting whatever argument the two were having, or wait and allow it to run its course.

"Everything all right?" Wilson had noticed his hesitation. Stepping up on to the porch to stand beside Lestrade, he cocked his head toward the door as the angry conversation caught his attention as well. Eyebrows shot up towards his helmet, and Wison turned to Lestrade. "May I?"

At Lestrade's nod, the man reached out and knocked on the door. Both voices suddenly went silent. A second later the door opened slightly, a sliver of a crack between door and frame allowing little more than a one-eyed glare framed by a furrowed brow and blotchy red skin.

Wilson smiled at the man as if the two were old friends. "Heard shouting," he said, his tone warm and friendly. "Just wanted to make sure everything was all right."

The door opened a little more, revealing the rest of the face; thick eyebrows smoothed out, though the rage never left the man's eyes, and the red that painted his face in angry blotches had yet to fade.

Lestrade remained still. He knew well enough the look of a man angry enough to be tempted by violence every bit as well as he knew the look of a man who often fell victim to that temptation.

"Everything's all right here." The man in question replied, attempting a smile and failing at it terribly. "Mum thinks I killed somebody. Asked the police to come question me about it." Catching sight of Lestrade, bushy eyebrows narrowed once again, this time in suspicion. "Who's that?" he demanded.

Wilson looked over at Lestrade, seemingly unbothered by the sharpness in the other man's tone. "That?" he asked, still casual, offering up another easy smile. "That would be the police, come to question you. Inspector Lestrade, at your service."

The constable threw a hand out, catching the door before it could slam in their faces. "Now, now," he chided, good humor never fading. "The man's just doing his job. The girl was killed here, up in her rooms, and he has to rule out anyone who has access to the building as a possible suspect before he can move on to finding the killer."

"What's he care?" the man wanted to know. "The girl was a whore. Everyone in the building knew it. Smiling at everyone, flirting with every man she set eyes on, leading good men on and then inviting those who are willing to stoop as low as to throw money on her up to her rooms. Surprised something didn't sooner."

Lestrade reached for his notebook and pencil, and the man startled. Wilson spared the inspector a brief glance before turning his attention back to the man at the door.

"Why don't you let us in, Danny?" he asked, voice gentle. "He's got a job to do, and the sooner he asks his questions, the sooner you and your mum will be left in peace."

"He's already writing, and he ain't even asked nothing yet," Danny grumbled. "Ought to close the door right in your faces."

"He's just trying to do his job, Danny," Wilson repeated. "Come on, lad, let us in."

Danny stepped back and opened the door. Wilson followed him in, Lestrade half a step behind him, and the three of them made their way to the kitchen.

"Ask your questions, then," Danny scowled at the inspector, folding his arms across his chest and shifting his weight as he brought himself up to his full height.

Lestrade was used to being shorter than other people. The action neither intimidated nor impressed him. "Right," he said, dark eyes dropping briefly to his notebook. "Where were you the night Alice Gardener was murdered?"

"Out." Lestrade raised an eyebrow and waited, pencil still as it pressed against paper. "Working. Not at the docks – I was helping out a friend."

"And the name of that friend?"

A hint of uncertainty leaked into the man's answer. "Jimmy Grey."

"He work the docks as well?" Wilson asked. Danny shook his head.

"He works for his father at the King's Head. Does odd jobs around the place, runs errands for him."

"And you two were running errands that night?" Lestrade asked. Danny nodded. "And he can verify that?" Another nod. "Aside from your obvious distaste for her...behavior towards men, how did you and Miss Gardener get along?"

"I was civil," the man all but sneered. "My mum raised me to be a gentleman."

"Did she ever flirt with you?" Lestrade asked. "You said she had a habit of leading men on. Were you one of those men?"

"Thought she was pretty when she moved in," Danny scoffed. "Before I knew what she was. After that, I wasn't interested." He looked almost smug as he looked the inspector up and down. "What about you, Inspector? That kind of woman interest you?"

"Danny," Wilson warned the other man, voice soft. Danny laughed.

"Just having a little fun," he said, shrugging. "Didn't mean nothing by it."

Lestrade handled the excuse the same way he had the question: by ignoring it. "I have a witness that claims you *were* interested, and that you didn't like that she was seeing someone else."

"Don't know anything about her seeing anybody." The man's good humor vanished instantly. "Don't know anybody stupid enough to fall in love with someone they gotta pay to be with."

"You were unaware she had a regular-caller?" Lestrade asked. "Your mother knew about it. Are you sure you didn't?"

"Mum's got a mouth on her," Danny growled. "She loves to gossip, and isn't particular about whether something's true or not when she passes it on. Hope you've got better information that what *she* told you."

"She says you're a good lad," Lestrade noted almost absently as he looked down at his notebook. "Other sources aren't so generous. She mistaken about that too?"

Danny took a step closer, face contorting. "Watch what you say about my mum."

Lestrade did not flinch. Wilson shifted, drawing the other man's attention.

"Don't mind the inspector. He's still getting used to the title," Wilson suggested, tone even as his eyes darted back and forth between the two men warily. "Trying to prove himself. Think about it, Danny. A girl gets murdered here on the East End, the older detectives can't be bothered so they send him to deal with it, thinking he'll write up a report and that'll be the end of it. Now he has to show them that he can handle the job, which means he has to find the girl's killer. If it makes him a little...overenthusiastic, who can blame him?"

"I've seen men stabbed and left dying in some side alley for less," Danny retorted, but he took a step back. "Just mind what you say about Mum."

"Of course," Wilson agreed. "He meant no disrespect."

Lestrade did not apologize. "Can you think of anyone who might have had a grudge against Miss Gardener?"

"No."

"Can you think of anyone she might have seen in the past who might have found out she was seeing someone else and gotten angry?"

"No."

Lestrade paused for half a second. "Did you know he wanted to marry her?"

"I knew."

"Did it make *you* angry?"

"No!" Wilson shifted as if to intervene again. Lestrade caught his eye and offered the constable a quick shake of the head. The constable settled.

"I have a witness who claims he'd caught you watching Miss Gardener in the past. That when he caught you at it you would 'scowl at him for a minute before retreating to the kitchen.' Another who described you as 'the sulky, surly sort' and 'not particularly friendly.'" Wilson did not so much as blink as Lestrade quoted part of their earlier conversation.

"And?" Danny demanded. "Not a crime to keep to myself."

"Or to stare at a pretty young woman?" Lestrade suggested.

"She *was* pretty," Danny snapped, scowling at the inspector. "A man tends to notice when a pretty girl walks by, but last time I checked, *that* wasn't a crime either."

Lestrade closed his notebook and returned it to his jacket pocket. "Thank you for your time," he said briskly. "We'll be in touch. Constable?"

Wilson blinked at him, but followed him willingly enough back outside.

"You may not remember, but I also said he stays out of trouble," the constable said as they stepped down into the street, tone mild. "Still, not a man I'd be in any kind of hurry to cross, Inspector."

Lestrade did not acknowledge the warning. "Can you tell me how to get to the King's Head?" he asked.

Wilson's eyebrows threatened to disappear under his helmet. "I can do better than that. Come on, I'll take you there myself. Less chance of you getting stabbed on the way," he added before the younger man could protest.

Twelve

They reached the King's Head without incident. Wilson paused outside the door briefly, steeling himself for the potential disaster that was to come. Piers, the owner, was a man who had been near-constant companions with hardship for most of his long life. He had a strong work ethic, a strong back, and a strong dislike for people who came into his pub looking to cause trouble.

They could very well be about to do just that, if not for the pub then for the man himself, depending on whether or not his son was involved in the poor girl's murder. At the very least, the man would be wary of a couple of policemen poking around, asking questions about his boy.

"Maybe tread softly on this one, Lestrade," he suggested as they headed inside. If the man heard him, it did not show; Lestrade took one step inside and looked around, eyes scanning the room with a focus that made more than a few patrons shift in their seats, whether out of nervous habit or simply to brace themselves for whatever excitement might follow in the wake of the King's Head's newest arrival.

Lestrade made straight for the bar, sidestepping people with an ease that suggested he was not only used to maneuvering around people who could not be bothered to watch where they were going, but had been doing so long enough that it had by now become nearly instinctual. Wilson followed at a more leisurely pace, allowing people time to notice the uniform, recognize the face beneath the helmet, and step out of the way.

He reached the bar only a few steps behind the inspector, smiling at Piers over the smaller man's shoulder.

Piers looked at Wilson, then down at Lestrade. "You two together?"

It came out more of a grunt than a question, and Wilson nodded. "This is Inspector Lestrade," he introduced the man before the pub's owner could start to get suspicious. "He's working the Gardener Case, that girl that got murdered over on Ratcliffe."

Piers nodded, then. "That what brings you here? The case?"

"Need to confirm an alibi," Lestrade spoke up. "For the landlady's son, Danny. Says he knows *your* son."

Piers' expression darkened. "My son didn't kill that girl." Lestrade was already shaking his head before the man even finished.

"Danny says he didn't either – that he was working a job with your son that night," Lestrade clarified quickly, a wise move on his part. The owner of the King's Head was not well known for his patience.

"I just need to confirm that Danny was with your son, and that they were where he said they were. Is your son here?"

"He's in the back," Piers nodded over his shoulder toward the back room before crossing over toward the doorway. Leaning through the open space, he shouted.

"Jimmy!"

A moment later his son came lumbering through, a younger but nearly exact copy of his father. "Wilson wants to ask you something. You tell him the truth, now."

James Grey looked from his father to the constable, worry clouding his features. "I didn't do nothing," he grunted.

"Didn't say you did," his father retorted. "Go on."

James looked around briefly, then nodded for them to follow him as he stepped out from behind the bar and over to a booth in the corner. "Makes people nervous, having the police standing at the bar like that," he said as he sat down.

"Of course," Lestrade agreed, taking a seat without prompting. "Inspector Lestrade. I'm looking into the murder of

Miss Alice Gardener over on Ratcliffe Highway. Where were you that night?"

"You think *I* did it?" James demanded, torn between shock and anger. "I don't even know the woman." He scowled at the inspector, and Wilson found himself once again preparing to intervene if necessary.

"But you recognize the name?" Lestrade prodded, and the man hesitated.

"I didn't – yes, I know who she is – Danny talks about her all the time, but we never spoke. I've never met the woman, only seen her in passing."

"While on the property."

"Yes."

"On the occasions you saw her, you were there meeting Danny?" Lestrade asked, reaching for his notebook. He received a nod in return. "So you know who she is, and you have access to the building. You understand I have to ask where you were on the night she was murdered, Mister Grey?"

When the other man simply stared at him he shrugged. "I have to eliminate anyone who currently has, or has in the past, had access to the building as a possible suspect. You know who she is, at least, even if you've never actually met, and you've been there before to meet up with Danny, so I have to ask where you were that night. If you weren't there and you can provide an alibi, I can mark you off the list and move on to someone else."

James was quiet for a moment, thinking the inspector's words over. Since the situation seemed to be under control, Wilson remained quiet as well, content to let the other man take the lead.

It was his investigation, after all.

"I was here that night. All night," James finally said. "We had a shipment come in. I worked the bar until close, and then my father and I spent most of the night unloading and unpacking it. Didn't finish up till nearly dawn."

"You and your father were here – anyone else with you?" Lestrade asked, eyes on paper as he made note of James's answer.

"Millie," the other man flushed slightly. "She stays sometimes while we unload, mostly as company, but she also helps with the lighter boxes." He looked across the bar. "That's her over there. Golden hair, sapphire eyes, rosy cheeks..."

Lestrade did not acknowledge James's sudden venture into more poetic territory. "I'll need to confirm with both of them." He paused for a fraction of a second. "Did you see anyone else that night?"

"No," James replied before asking, "Why?"

"What about Danny? Did he stop by?"

James's eyes narrowed. "Why? What are you implying?"

Lestrade shook his head. "I'm simply asking if anyone else stopped by that night."

"Danny might have been by," James looked uncertain. "If he says he was here, I'm sure he was at some point. Did he say when?"

"Did he stop by for a drink?" Lestrade asked rather than answer the question. "To talk? Maybe he helped with the shipment?"

"Did he say he helped?"

Lestrade set his notebook and pencil down almost reverently before looking back up and all but skewering the other man with his gaze. "Danny claims the two of you were out running errands the night Alice Gardener was killed."

James blinked. "I was here all night. Ask Millie. Ask my father. We were here until morning, unloading. I never left to run any errands." He said, voice flat, expression strained.

"And Danny?"

James turned away. "I would have remembered, if he had stopped by."

It took less than a quarter of an hour to confirm James's story with both his father Piers, and Millie, the serving girl. The boy's father came over almost as soon as James left, and quickly confirmed his son had been telling the truth. Shortly after he left, the serving girl came over, winking at Wilson and asking if she could get either of them a drink.

"I'll have a pint of my usual," Wilson decided. He was off duty, technically had been for a few hours now, and even if he hadn't been no one would have said anything. There were a few constables local to the East End who pretty much started and ended their shifts here, and nobody bothered *them,* and at least one old timer whom Wilson had yet to see in uniform and sober at the same time in all the years he had known the man.

Wilson was known here well enough that no one would bat an eye at him having a drink, and that no one would consider a constable nursing a pint after a long day an easy mark. Nor would they bother Lestrade, at least not while the inspector was with him, even if there had been more than a few wary glances thrown his way since their arrival.

Millie turned to Lestrade, who simply blinked.

"You working, or going home after this?" Walker asked, prompting the younger man to turn and stare at him. "He'll have the same, my dear," Wilson answered for him. The man could drink it or not, it was all the same to him, but at least Millie would not be stuck standing there while he sorted the matter out.

Lestrade recovered enough to reclaim his notebook and pencil from the table and tuck it away into his jacket pocket, but apparently not enough to do-or say-anything else. Wilson was hardly bothered; he could handle a little silence now and again, and Lestrade seemed to need a minute, though the constable had no idea what had set him off.

Millie returned fairly quickly with their drinks, flashing Lestrade a mischievous grin as she set down his drink purely, Wilson thought, for the simple pleasure of seeing the man flustered. He offered her a stiff nod in return before reaching for his pint.

The man took exactly one sip before setting it down and ignoring it.

Wilson shrugged and turned his attention to his own glass.

"You think Danny did it?" Wilson was halfway through his pint before he felt any inclination toward breaking the silence between them.

Lestrade blinked, then shrugged, something in those dark eyes flickering briefly before settling down. The man was a difficult read at times, even for Wilson, but he suspected whatever he had just seen had something to do with the not-so-subtle way the inspector's eyes scanned the room before coming back to focus on Wilson.

"He doesn't have an alibi," Lestrade said, voice low.

"Or he has one, but didn't want to tell us the truth," Walker offered. It was unlikely the man had one and simply not wanted to tell them, but not entirely impossible.

Lestrade tilted his head in acknowledgment. "Either way, he lied."

"Are you going back tonight?" Wilson wanted to know. Lestrade shook his head. "Well, when you do, be careful. Danny may have managed to stay out of trouble so far, but as I said before, he hangs out with a rough bunch, and he's not exactly helpless on his own. He works down at the docks, mostly heavy lifting, and the boy's got some muscle on him. Say the wrong thing, insult his mother, for example, and trouble he may be."

Lestrade accepted the warning without comment. "I'll most likely stop tomorrow morning," he admitted. "It's getting late."

"It is," Wilson agreed. "We need to think about getting you back where you belong. The East End is hardly welcoming during the day, Lestrade. After dark..." he trailed off, leaving the thought unfinished, and wondering whether it was the foolish pride of youth that caused the other man to entirely fail to express even a modicum of concern, or something else entirely.

Whatever it was, Wilson breathed a sigh of relief as he sent the man on his way less than an hour later. Arrogance or experience or whatever else aside, the man could be intense at times, and after a while it had started to grate on the older man, leaving him tense and uneasy.

It was a relief to get home and finally get out of uniform, and to be able to get off his tired and aching feet. It had been a long day, and while a lot of the fault for that had been his own, Wilson had been reluctant to leave the still fairly fresh inspector to his own devices, particularly after dark.

He made a note to check in on the man tomorrow, if not personally, then by having one of the other constables familiar with Ratcliffe Highway keep an eye out. He figured an inspector who actually cared about finding the person responsible for the murder of a single mother of two who had, at times, more than dabbled in prostitution was enough of a novelty to attract notice.

Thirteen

"Lestrade?" the inspector in question paused in the hallway long enough for Smith to catch up. "Any luck with the Gardener case?"

Lestrade did not ask whether Smith's question was about whether or not he had found the murderer or had found someone to take the children still in Smith's care, but he did take a moment to consider before choosing simply to answer the question presented. "The landlady's son lied about where he was that night. He says he wasn't interested in her, but another witness suggests otherwise."

"Her lover?" Smith asked, and Lestrade nodded. "He was in here the other day, wasn't he?" Another nod. "I don't suppose he could have been trying to make the other man look bad?"

"Wouldn't explain why the son lied," Lestrade countered with a shrug.

"I suppose not." Smith conceded. "Going back today?"

"I'm on my way now." Lestrade hesitated, looking the other man over. "Anything else?"

"No, just checking in." Smith looked mildly uncomfortable, a rare enough occurrence for the man based on the admittedly short time Lestrade had known him.

"Something wrong with the children?" Lestrade asked, though he had no idea what he was going to do if Smith said he could not keep them anymore. He still had yet to find anyone willing to take them in.

Smith shifted uncomfortably, opened his mouth as if to answer the question, then shrugged. "Nothing wrong at all," he said, voice thoughtful. An expression that Lestrade could not decipher briefly crossed his face before disappearing behind an easy smile. "They seem to be doing just find, and the wife still has yet to get tired of them running about, so I figure you've still got time to figure out what to do with them."

Lestrade nodded absently, a thought beginning to form, but a constable calling his name redirected his attention, and the idea was lost before it could fully take shape.

"Message for you, sir." The constable held out a folded sheet of paper that looked as if it had been hastily torn from a notebook. Lestrade accepted it, opening the note to find an equally hastily scrawled message inside.

It took him a moment to decipher the untidy scrawl, but once he had, he tucked the note away before turning back to Smith.

"There's been a new development," Lestrade told the older inspector. "If you'll excuse me."

"I'll come along, if you don't mind," Smith fell into step beside him as he started down the hall. "Last time you had that look it meant trouble."

"The note was from Constable Wilson," Lestrade replied tersely. "Alice Gardener's landlady was assaulted sometime last night; he thinks it was the son."

"The one who lied about his alibi?" Smith asked, and Lestrade nodded.

Constable Wilson was in the kitchen with the woman when Lestrade and Smith got there, tending to a kettle on the stove while the woman sat nearby in a chair borrowed from the table. Face battered, the woman looked up as the two inspectors entered the room.

"Haven't you done enough?" she spat at Lestrade, her tone pure venom. "My boy Danny would *never-*"

"Hurt a soul?" Lestrade asked, tone dry, and the woman looked away.

"I can't believe it," she murmured. "I can't believe he'd do such a thing."

Wilson turned away from the stove to press a fresh cup of tea into the woman's hands. "Danny didn't like us coming around asking questions yesterday," he offered to Lestrade, his own voice soft. "Or when his mother asked him if he knew anything about the poor girl after we'd left."

"He has a temper, but he didn't *kill* that girl," Danny's mother insisted.

"Where is he now?" Lestrade asked. Again the woman looked away. "He lied about where he was the night she was killed. Why would he lie, if he didn't do it?" When he received no response the inspector sighed. "He was angry enough, last night, to assault his own mother," he pressed. "If he felt he'd been rejected, or made a fool of by the Gardener woman, if he'd found out she was seeing another man regularly and got jealous, how angry would he be? Angry enough to kill?"

"Is he at work?" Wilson asked gently. "At the docks?"

The barest tilt of the head in confirmation. "I did my best to raise him right," she said. "I tried so hard to make sure he didn't turn out like his father."

"You did everything you could," Wilson told her. "Will you be all right?"

"Leave me," the woman sniffed once before bracing herself and getting to her feet. "I have a lot of work to get done, and you lot are in the way. Go on," her voice hardened. "Do what you have to do."

They made their way down to the docks without incident, largely in part to Constable Wilson's familiarity with both the area, and its people. Smith found himself flanked on both sides as they approached the docks: Wilson on one side, Lestrade on the other, and while he could understand easily enough the older constable putting himself between the inspector and possible mischief, he found the fact that Lestrade seemed to be attempting to do the same on his other side more than a bit amusing, at least until a ragged child wandered a bit too close.

Lestrade caught the small hand mere seconds before it could successfully snake its way into his pocket, but let go willingly enough when the would-be pickpocket tried to break free. A second later the child was gone, disappeared into the crowd. Neither Lestrade nor Wilson reacted to the incident, though Smith decided he was fine being in the middle, and stored the incident away for later perusal.

Their suspect clocked them the second they came into view, dropping his half of a large crate-much to his coworker's dismay and making a break for it. He shoved past another colleague in his haste, nearly knocking the man down.

Smith and Lestrade took off after him. Out of the corner of his eye, Smith noted as Wilson split off, presumably in an attempt to cut the man off farther down; he probably knew the area better than either inspector.

Less familiar with their current surroundings, Smith and Lestrade had to resort to keeping the man in sight while trying to dodge any obstacles in their way.

Lestrade ducked under a long crate being carried by no less than four men without so much as blinking, but Smith was forced to go around. Angry swearing followed him as he brushed against one of the men, but he didn't have time to look back, let alone apologize.

They were gaining on their suspect, inch by inch; Smith had only gotten a brief glimpse of the man before he fled, but in that short moment he had not given off the impression of a man built for long-distance running. Smith was gaining on Lestrade as well, most likely only because of the younger man's shorter stride. He suspected, however, that if put to the test Lestrade could outlast him.

Smith nearly careened into another overly large crate, losing precious seconds in recovering his balance, and by that time both Lestrade and the man they were after had disappeared around the corner.

Lestrade heard a shout of warning as he rounded the corner and ducked just in time to avoid getting hit in the face. His would-be assailant swore as Lestrade turned back toward him. Sweat dripping, face contorted into a scowl, he turned as if to escape back the way they had just come only for Smith to catch up, blocking his exit.

Apparently deciding he had a better chance against Lestrade, the man turned back to face the younger inspector.

"Don't do it," Wilson warned. "You're outnumbered *and* surrounded, Danny."

Smith simply waited.

Danny raised his fists, lunging forward and throwing a punch that Lestrade sidestepped easily, catching his opponent in the stomach with a well-placed jab of his own as he dodged the attack. Danny doubled over, stumbling briefly, then straightened up as he turned to face Lestrade once more.

His second attempt swung wide, and Lestrade simply ducked. Popping back up he caught the man in the face with his own fist, and with that it was all over.

A second later Danny was bent over and clutching at his nose. Blood dripped from his hands; Lestrade was fairly certain he had broken it. The man put up no more resistance as Lestrade moved in, fastening a pair of handcuffs on his wrists before offering his handkerchief.

The look Danny fixed him with was one of pure hatred, but he accepted the handkerchief anyway, bringing it up to press against his nose.

"You're under arrest for the murder of Alice Gardener," Lestrade said as the other two policemen joined them.

Fourteen

"Got a minute?" Lestrade looked up from writing to find Inspector Smith hovering in his doorway, his expression uneasy. He set aside his pencil and gestured for the other man to come in.

Smith entered, taking a seat across from Lestrade and bracing himself as if for a difficult conversation. The action was unusual for him, as was the current tension in his frame-Smith was usually fairly easygoing-and it left the younger inspector unsettled.

"Adams said that Danny confessed to the murder of Miss Gardener?" he asked, a bit awkwardly, and Lestrade nodded.

"He did. His mother also admitted that he had, in fact, been in the habit of watching the woman, whenever he was around. And complaining about the visitors she received."

"And her lover?" Smith asked, and Lestrade took a moment to study the man before him.

"He's willing to testify to the same." Smith nodded, looked around the office for a moment, then took a deep breath.

"Any luck with the children?" he asked, and Lestrade shook his head.

"Their grandparents won't take them," he said bluntly. "I haven't been able to find any other family members, anyone else willing to take them in." He resisted the urge to sigh; part of him had known that the chances of finding someone were next to nothing. The options he was left with, though…

"About that," Smith said, shifting in his seat and looking almost sheepish. "The missus and I were talking, and she's-well, she's pretty much gotten used to having them about. That is, I think she's been hoping it would take a while to find a home for them, and I'm pretty sure it's going to hit pretty hard when-if you do, and…" Lestrade waited, one eyebrow lifting almost on its own as he tried to sort out what the other man was trying to say.

Smith took another deep breath. "What I mean to say, Lestrade, is that the missus has gone and gotten more than a bit attached, and I'm pretty sure it would break her heart to see them go." He paused, then added softly, "Might have gotten a bit attached myself."

Lestrade blinked. Taking a minute to consider the option, then another to study the man before him, he asked, "Are you sure about this?"

Smith nodded. "We, uh, we haven't been able to have any of our own," he admitted. "It's been hard on her, and now that she's been looking after the little ones, well." He cleared his throat.

The confession made Lestrade uncomfortable. "If you're willing to take them in, I don't see why you couldn't." He hesitated. "Have you mentioned this to the children?" he asked.

"I didn't want to get their hopes up, though Rosie keeps sighing and declaring she wishes she could stay with us forever." He cleared his throat again. "And then the missus gets a little teary-eyed, and little William runs over to give her a big hug. I don't think the children would be against it, if that's what you're worried about, though you're welcome to stop by and see for yourself."

Lestrade shook his head. "I don't think that will be necessary," he said. Looking back down at the paperwork on his desk in an attempt to hide his relief-and gratitude-he finally asked, "Anything else I can do for you?"

Smith laughed. "I think that will be all for now, Lestrade," he said. Getting up from his chair, he excused himself, grinning and shaking his head as he left.

Lestrade went back to filling out his report.

Milton Keynes UK
Ingram Content Group UK Ltd.
UKHW031841121024
449535UK00010B/584